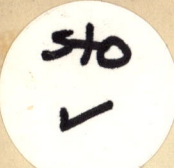

FRIENDS OF ACPL

S0-ERS-481

THE HAPPY ANIMALS
OF ATAGAHI

ATAGAHI

THE HAPPY ANIMALS OF ATAGAHI

By
BESSIE ROWLAND JAMES

Illustrated by
W. R. LOHSE

THE BOBBS-MERRILL COMPANY
PUBLISHERS
INDIANAPOLIS   NEW YORK

Copyright, 1935
By The Bobbs-Merrill Company

First Edition

Printed in the United States of America

PRINTED AND BOUND BY
BRAUNWORTH & CO., INC.
BOOK MANUFACTURERS
BROOKLYN, NEW YORK

U. S. 735916

For
CHINCHEE

Buckingham. C o

Acknowledgment . . .

These stories were suggested by the Indian myths found in numerous reports of the Bureau of Ethnology of the Smithsonian Institution. I have written them solely to entertain, attempting to build, I hope, a lively book around the Indian lore of the woods and the animals. Where it was possible to do so, I have followed the original myths. Anyone familiar with them knows that many are unsuitable for children. As the book is intended for younger readers—and listeners—I have interpreted incidents in modern terms and with modern symbols of their little world which they understand best.

B. R. J.

CONTENTS

CHAPTER		PAGE
I	Atagahi	9
II	The Giant Flint	16
III	Rabbit Scatters Flint to the Winds	29
IV	The First Fire	48
V	Rabbit and Possum Lose Their Tails	65
VI	Tournament Day	87
VII	The Crawfish and the Great Buzzard	105
VIII	Rabbit Tricks the Tie Snakes	126
IX	Turkey's Singing Lesson	147
X	Rabbit Shows Wildcat	161
XI	Wolf Upsets Terrapin	175
XII	The Rescue of Rabbit	188
XIII	Rabbit Is Banished to the Island	209
XIV	Terrapin's Trick	233

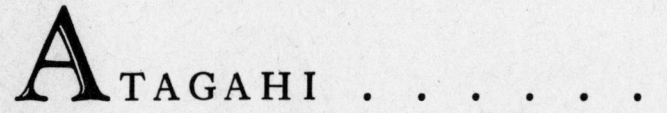

The Happy Animals of Atagahi

Chapter I

Atagahi . . . .

HIGH up and far away in the wildest depths of the Great Smoky Mountains of Tennessee and North Carolina is the happy land of Atagahi* where the contented animals live. No living person has ever been there because the trees and briers have grown up thickly around it, tangling themselves into an impenetrable wall that encloses Atagahi and shuts it away from trespassers. This is the reason that the animals are contented.

The Indians who used to live close by in the lowlands tell many tales of Atagahi. How they discovered Atagahi they do not say. Perhaps long ago, before the trees became so dense, a scout strayed there and brought back the stories to the tribe. The Indians named Atagahi, which means enchanted, and composed songs and ceremonial dances in honor of birds and beasts and even insects which dwell there.

---
*A Cherokee word pronounced Ata-ga'-hi (Ahta-gah'-he).

Certainly, from what the Indians tell, Atagahi must be a magical land. By daylight, they say, bears and mountain lions pad boldy down to the shores of Lake Atagahi for their long drink of water. They have never heard the crash of the hunter's gunshot and,

unlike their frightened brethren of the Outside World, do not slink about in darkness and leave behind them pictures of many footprints to obscure their trail.

And the birds likewise are unafraid. Battalions of ducks and white-fronted geese whir and drill uninterruptedly above the lake and Bald Eagle perches serenely on Pilot Knob, for in Atagahi they know those ugly tales of children snatched away to his mountain home and devoured are untrue. Bald Eagle loves fish and eats little else. Yet, the world over, he is known as a dangerous, evil bird and this undeserved reputation gave his face that melancholy expression and turned his head white before he was four years old.

In Atagahi Black Bear is the leader of the animals because he is wise and fearless and for him the waters of the lake are magic medicine. If he cuts his foot he has merely to dip it into the lake to be healed, which does not happen with any of the other animals. They must go to Skunk and take his smelly medicine. But Skunk seems to work magic with his patients. More often than not a whiff of his medicine brings about an instant cure, causing the invalid to race off with extraordinary vigor. In this way much sickness in Atagahi is avoided.

The magic lake has a legend. They say that long ago in the fall of the year when the animals were burning the grass a poplar tree caught fire. After the tree was destroyed the earth around it began to burn. Day after day the fire continued, eating a great hole in the ground, and the animals were powerless to stop it. In sadness and alarm they prepared to leave their beloved Atagahi when White Bear, the Guardian of the North, came to visit his brother Black Bear.

"Do not worry," White Bear told the animals. "The Ice Man who lives in the North is my friend.

He is the enemy of fire. I will ask him to put out this fire."

White Bear hurriedly returned to his home and very soon the Ice Man sent a snowstorm which halted the fire. In the spring the snow melted and the great hole was filled with water. This is Lake Atagahi and the animals with far-hearing ears say they can catch the sound of crackling embers beneath it.

Near the magic lake in a clearing is the Chopped Oak before which the animals hold their council meetings. Black Bear is their leader in the same way that a chief is the leader of an Indian tribe, but whenever there is something important to decide the animals gather in council and say how they wish it done. After the meeting Woodpecker flies to the Chopped Oak and carves another notch on its ancient trunk which is dotted with the record of many councils.

Every inhabitant of Atagahi has his station and duties. There is Bullfrog, for instance. He is the Marshal and his honking "CRO-OAK!" calls the council meetings to order. Rabbit, who darts about so swiftly, is the Messenger for the animals and busy little Wren for the birds. Cricket, because of his sharp jaws, is the Barber.

Although his reputation has saddened him, Bald Eagle after all is a very fortunate bird. His title is

Guardian of the Upper Regions and his duties provide him with a beautiful view. Sitting on Pilot Knob he can see all at one time the magic lake, Chopped Oak, Mulberry Place, Hickory Nut Gap and Talking Rock. Bald Eagle likes to watch the River Path which is as lively as the main street of any village. Few of the animals drink at the lake. Most of them prefer the River and so they are bobbing up and down this trail at all hours.

Up on Blood Mountain, so called because its soil is rosy red, Bald Eagle can see where the River begins. First it is a trickle of rainwater born of the last downpour. Here and there among the rocks and the laurels and rhododendrons it plays hide-and-seek and discovers its cousins dribbling down the mountainside. Together they splash ahead, a swifter, stronger current, and tumble recklessly over a ledge to become a dancing, foamy waterfall.

From the waterfall pours the Mountain Stream which bumps and stumbles over a lane of stones in a headlong rush to reach a quieter existence on the plains where it turns into the lazy River. But just before achieving this calm, the Stream churns through one last violent ordeal among the Haunted Whirlpools. The Indians' story is that once some bears with their usual curiosity dove into the spinning circles for a swim. They came out reeling and vowing someone lived in the whirlpools who slapped them and turned them round and round. And so now none of the animals ever goes near the Haunted Whirlpools to swim, not even the bears.

A short way from the whirlpools and in the middle of the River is the Island which is spoken of in whispers and with shudders of fear. It's a dreadful place and the grubworms live there. When one of his tribe is especially bad, Black Bear sends him to the Island as a punishment, and the grubworms do not like having an exile among them any more than an animal cares to live with grubworms. Many years past, when a strange sickness visited Atagahi and killed many of the animals, a grubworm said:

"Well, I don't care if the animals are dying. There'll be fewer of them to trod on us."

And the grubworm began to laugh and, shaking with joy, she lost her balance and fell over backward. Since then grubworms, as a penalty for their ancestor's unsympathetic remark, have wriggled along upside down, which has not increased their affection for animals. But after they began to crawl in this uncomfortable fashion, Black Bear considerately had them all collected and transported to the Island where there are no heavy-footed animals, unless a prisoner is sent over. This rarely occurs for the memory of the wriggling little creature that was made happy by their deaths has many times kept the animals from misbehaving.

A pleasanter spot on the River is Frogtown, al-

though very noisy. The animals go there for amusement and they play a game, scoring a point each time they actually see a frog leap into the water. This is not easy. The frogs of Frogtown dive through the air quicker than the eye can follow them and only by their *plop!* when they hit the River is it known they have jumped.

Of these places and many others you hear in the stories the Indians tell of the contented animals of Atagahi. There is one which relates how Rabbit was chosen to drive the giant Flint from the mountain.

Chapter II

THE GIANT FLINT . . . .

FLINT was the only giant who lived in Atagahi and the animals often said, "Thank goodness, there are no more. Flint gives us enough trouble."

Luckily the giant's home was somewhere near the top of Blood Mountain. This kept most of the smaller animals from ever crossing his path, but that still left the deer, the antelopes, the mountain lions and the bears who climbed high to graze, and they knew Flint well—too well, as was told by the ugly, bald scars that streaked their fur coats.

For a very long time the animals' leaders had tried to drive Flint from Atagahi, but getting rid of a giant is not so easy, especially with only two ways of reaching the Outside World. One way was to fly, as the birds did, and the other was to squeeze through a small opening in the wall of trees and briers, as the animals rarely bothered to do. The idea of getting this monster who weighed tons and tons and had no wings to soar into the sky vault was preposterous, even if Flint himself had been willing to try it; which he wasn't for he too was contented in Atagahi. As for the opening in the wall, perhaps if he had squeezed very hard, he might have pushed one of his big feet through; but he wouldn't do this for Flint wasn't interested in squeezing. He had an enormous appetite and he loved bulging.

With annoying hardihood he survived all plots to lure him to destruction and after this there was scarcely anything more to try. About all the animals could hope for was that some day the disagreeable giant would grow old and stop tormenting them.

But Flint appeared ageless as he strode over the mountain in his noisily clanking clothes looking for victims. It was his monstrous costume that gave the animals their scars. Sticking out all over it were points that could jab like sharp blades. Flint's trick was to hide in the tall grass, spread his clothing carefully so that each sharp point stood up, and wait for a grazing animal to come along and stumble over him. Then his booming laughter would roar like thunder over the mountain as he watched a terrified deer dashing away, or perhaps a bear limping off howling with pain.

Black Bear was distressed by the sufferings of the

animals and sought vainly for a means of preventing them. One morning he decided to go up Blood

Mountain and pay Flint a visit. Somehow he hoped to persuade him to change his ways.

After a long hot climb he found the giant stretched out in the grass, his eyes glinting with evil expectancy as he heard an animal approaching. But Black Bear fooled him. He took care not to stumble, and Flint was sorely disappointed.

"Gosh!" he said in disgust. "I don't know what's

getting into animals these days. It's getting harder all the time to scare them and as for stumbling, they seem to be learning how to keep out of my way. I don't like it one little bit."

"Oh, you still scare us, Flint, and plenty of the animals get hurt," said Black Bear sadly.

"Do I really?" asked Flint with delight. "I'm glad to hear that. I've been worrying lately about whether I was losing my knack."

"Not at all, as far as I can see," said Black Bear. "That's what I'm here to talk about. When you hear one of us coming, why don't you shout a warning? You could still have the fun of scaring us, but if you yelled no one would get hurt. You could yell, 'Look out for Flint!'"

The giant stared in surprise. "But why should I yell?" he demanded. "I'd rather hear one of you animals yell."

"I'll instruct them to yell," said Black Bear.

"Yeah, but I wouldn't care for yells like that," said Flint. "I like shrieks of pain. They're entertaining."

Black Bear said that if entertainment was all Flint wanted, he'd be glad to send up some animals every morning who would keep him amused for the day.

"Thanks," said the giant scornfully. "I can entertain myself."

And to every other proposal Black Bear made he coldly said, "No," or else he laughed like the rumbling of thunder. Flint brought the interview to an end by announcing that he was working on a new costume for himself and it would have longer, sharper points.

"Longer, sharper points!" exclaimed Black Bear in horror, and he never said another word to Flint after that, but went stamping off down the mountain in a terrible rage.

He was still stamping and raging when he reached home, and he summoned Rabbit and Wren and sent them off with messages calling the council to meet in four days.

Through the filmy dawn of the fourth morning the animals flocked over the paths leading to the Chopped Oak. They were tramping in even from the long distances, like Beaver who lived on the River far downstream. It would be a big council. This was because the messengers had spread the word through the woods, along the water and among the trees that Black Bear was in a fury. Everybody was curious to know what had made him so angry. Never before had he lost his temper and usually he punished the animals who did.

"Now who'll punish Black Bear?" Terrapin asked as he plodded tediously toward the meeting place. Terrapin asked everyone that passed him—and this *was* everyone—but nobody paid any attention to his extraordinary inquiry. He was always saying such foolish things and long ago the animals had found out there weren't any answers to most of his questions. But Ground Squirrel came by after a time and she paused because she could not believe what her ears heard.

"Who'll punish Black Bear?" she repeated in amazement. "Why, Terrapin, where did you get such an idea?"

A pleased expression swept across Terrapin's small face. "Oh, I have lots of ideas," he boasted and added defiantly, "even if some say I can't get an idea through my thick shell."

"You should have kept this one out, for it is not a brilliant idea," Ground Squirrel commented gravely. "Couldn't you get rid of it quickly and quietly?"

Terrapin twisted his neck and considered. "Well, I might, if someone gave me an answer," he conceded. "I do need something in my head. I don't like that empty feeling. I'd love an answer for a change." And he sighed wistfully.

Ground Squirrel's head tilted sideward sympathetically. "Poor Terrapin," she said and stroked his shell with a dainty paw. "You do have your troubles, but you'll have more of them if you go around asking,

'Who'll punish Black Bear?' That's disrespectful."

"But who *will* punish him, Ground Squirrel? Please give me an answer."

"I can't give you an answer, Terrapin, because there isn't any. Black Bear is our leader. We all love him. He's the wisest, kindest leader we've ever had. Old Man Flint must have acted pretty badly to make Black Bear so angry. He's a wicked, mean, old giant and——"

"Stop! Stop!" shrieked Terrapin.

With startled eyes Ground Squirrel glanced apprehensively behind her. She saw nothing there to be afraid of, or anything elsewhere. Puzzled, her gaze returned to Terrapin. His head rolled around on his neck as if he were in agony. "What's wrong, Terrapin?" she asked anxiously.

"Ooooo!" moaned Terrapin, shutting his eyes tightly and wrinkling up his face, as if he had tasted something disagreeable. "Ooooo! Words, words, words. They make my head ache. Everybody talks too much. I can't understand all the words. You start talking about Black Bear and then before I know it you're talking about Flint. I can't keep it straight. Ooooo!"

Ground Squirrel took a deep breath and prepared to explain once more. "There is no answer," she said simply to him. "Nobody'll punish Black Bear."

At this Terrapin began to bounce excitedly on his four short legs and scream, "That's it! That's it! That's it!"

Ground Squirrel stared in bewilderment and waited for Terrapin to quiet down. She knew he tired easily. And shortly Terrapin was winded and ceased to bounce.

"That's it!" he repeated hoarsely, gasping for breath. "The answer is nobody. *Question*———" Terrapin looked blank; he was trying to remember. "*Question*—what was the question, Ground Squirrel? Oh, never mind. I don't need a question any more. I've got an answer. *Answer*. Nobody. Thank you, Ground Squirrel, for an answer. I haven't had one in a long while. It feels so good in my head. *Answer*. Nobody."

Ground Squirrel tightened her lips to hold back an amused smile. Of course, she didn't want to offend Terrapin, especially when everything seemed to be working out so nicely. She twitched her tail impatiently and said, "Don't you think we ought to be hurrying along to the meeting? It's getting late."

"Nobody. *Answer*. Nobody," murmured Terrapin. He had not heard what Ground Squirrel said, but presently she had him moving slowly toward the Chopped Oak. Terrapin traveled the trail in a trance.

"Nobody, nobody," he continued to mutter quietly.

Terrapin always is the last to arrive anywhere and so he and Ground Squirrel straggled into the council after all the animals had seated themselves in a circle around Black Bear and Marshal Bullfrog. Terrapin directed his unsteady steps to where his friend Rabbit crouched.

"Rabbit, what do you think?" he asked exuberantly. "I've got an answer. It's nobody!"

"Ssssh!" said Rabbit and frowned because Bullfrog was puffing out his throat.

"C-R-R-OAK! C-R-R-OAK!" honked the Marshal, and the council came to order.

Black Bear started in right off to tell of his visit to Flint. "And Flint is going to have a new suit of clothes with longer, sharper points that will cause us more pain," he concluded. "We have got to do something to take the giant out of Atagahi before he puts on his new clothes!"

"Yes! Yes!" the animals roared and squeaked, and some clapped their paws to show they agreed.

"I've been wondering what to do," Black Bear said. "It's a hard proposition. It will do no good to send the strongest animal against Flint because he is bigger and stronger than any of us. I think we might try sending our cleverest and perhaps he can outwit Flint and trick him into doing something that will take him away from Atagahi forever. Now the question is who'll we send?"

"Nobody," Terrapin promptly answered, and everyone scowled at him, which made Terrapin feel so badly that he popped his head inside his shell where he couldn't see faces with disapproving expressions.

"I think Rabbit is the animal to choose. Sometimes he can be very, very clever," said Black Bear.

"Hooray! Hooray!" squealed the smaller animals.

Only a few of the larger ones roared because not many were acquainted with Rabbit. He belonged among the smaller animals who knew his clever ways and admired him. But, day after day in the woods, big animals passed by Rabbit without a nod or a greeting, their heads so far above him that their eyes didn't catch sight of him. And Rabbit so wanted to be on speaking terms with all the big animals. It hurt his pride to be ignored. Once he had tried to attract the attention of Wolf by lying down right across his path, expecting at least to be stepped on. Instead Wolf carefully stepped over him, as if he were a stone, and went on his way without a word.

Black Bear's words, though, made everyone, big and little, turn their eyes toward Rabbit. Rabbit sat up very straight, his chest swelling with pride, and looked as important as he knew how. He started to push his chin forward, but that hurt since he had such a tiny

chin, and so instead he stretched his neck and held his head higher.

"Rabbit, will you go up the mountain and see if you are smart enough to drive Flint out of Atagahi?" Black Bear asked.

Rabbit stood up and shook out his long fluffy tail, for this was before he had lost his long tail. It oc-

The Giant Flint

curred to him that he ought to make a speech. This was indeed an opportunity. A very fine speech would keep the big animals from ever forgetting him. And here was another piece of luck! Puma was stretched out on the ground almost at his feet. Rabbit could make his speech looking *down* on a big animal!

Thus inspired Rabbit opened his mouth to begin and at the same instant Puma opened his. A long, loud yawn emerged. The mountain lion brought his lips together again with a satisfied smack, curled himself into a snug ball and closed his eyes. He had prowled all night. Daybreak was his bedtime. Puma went to sleep.

But he had spoiled Rabbit's fine speech.

"Well, I'll do the best I can against Flint," Rabbit said, this being all he remembered of what he wanted to say.

"Hip! Hip! Hooray! Hooray for Rabbit!"

The animals, large and small, jumped up and down, stamped their feet, roared, bellowed, snorted, screaked and screeched. Those with long tails waved them. The noise was terriffic, so loud it hurt the ears to listen, but Rabbit did not mind. He listened with pleasure. The big animals were making the most noise. Rabbit smiled and bowed. The noise increased because Puma awakened and began to howl.

"C-R-R-OAK! C-R-R-OAK!" The Marshal honked for silence.

The council was quiet.

"Let's get our work done," said Black Bear. "We'll shout when Flint's out of the way. Rabbit, can you start up the mountain today? I'd like no more of us hurt."

"I'll go now," Rabbit said, "but I don't know what I can do to Flint."

"Then start now and you can be thinking all the time you're climbing," said Black Bear. "But be careful. I'll advise you not to eat anything on the mountain. You might forget about Flint and get hurt. I wish you luck. Good-by."

Rabbit scampered out of the circle of animals and darted toward the woods where the mountain begins.

"Good-by, Rabbit, good luck," he heard the animals calling after him.

"Good-by." That was Terrapin.

"Good-by." That was Ground Squirrel.

"GOOD-BY." That was Puma.

Chapter III

Rabbit Scatters Flint to the Winds

Rabbit spent a tiresome day on the mountain looking for Flint. In the morning he had raced along happily, remembering the cheering and that Black Bear had picked him from among all the animals and said he was very clever. He felt extraordinarily alive and important and ideas for banishing the giant from Atagahi clicked through his head, although he did not settle on a real plan. But after he rushed from the council Rabbit did not meet a soul and the quiet on the mountain made him feel dreadfully lonesome. Rabbit was used to being frightened by noises, but now that he heard no noises the silence frightened him, and so by the middle of the afternoon he had lost his high spirits and his brain was dull.

Hours had gone by without his even hearing a startling sound to cause him to twist his ears, or to quiver his nose and sniff to find out where the danger came from. Nothing happened to make his legs leap to bear him away to a safe hiding-place. Now these are the little things, as everyone knows, which make a rabbit the sort of animal he is and, when the silence had lasted for a long, long while, Rabbit was not surprised that his skin started trembling queerly. He was beginning to feel as if he weren't a rabbit any more.

"Cabbages and lettuce leaves!" he exclaimed in dismay, for Rabbit enjoyed being a rabbit.

He whirled around and sprang over the top of a laurel bush. The jump stopped the twitch in his legs, but his body could not be still. He bounded over the laurel again. His legs were in fine shape now, but the rest of him was shaking itself out of shape.

"What'll I do? What'll I do?" Rabbit asked desperately.

Holding his head between his forepaws, he sat on his hind legs and thought, which was not at all necessary. Rabbit knew exactly what he should do, but he did not want to take his medicine. What he needed was a large dose of noise. He hadn't had a good fright all day, a serious matter in the life of an animal who is used to jumping at every sound.

The quivers returned to his legs. Now Rabbit had to take his medicine. He got behind a rock and gave it a shove. The rock rolled over slowly, but with a few turns went tumbling down the mountain faster and faster. Rabbit heard it clattering out of sight. Next he heard a frightful BUMP! His ears twirled on his head and his nose wrinkled and sniffed. The bump had been loud and it smelled dangerous. With a scared leap Rabbit scurried farther up the mountain.

He ran until he had to rest and then hid behind a tree. His ears pointed backward, forward and sideward listening. His nose was going sniff, sniff, sniff, in time with the fast beat of his heart. He heard nothing and smelled nothing.

Boldly Rabbit stepped from behind the tree.

"Dear me, what an awful scare that was," he said and tossed his head jauntily. But where was Flint? It was getting late. The Sun was deepening to the ruddy shade of late afternoon, as Rabbit could see, and he had done nothing about the giant. The sunset was very lovely and Rabbit sat up on his haunches to admire the colors in the sky. Suddenly his body stiffened.

"Cabbages and lettuce leaves! Oh my!" he exclaimed. "I'm looking straight at the Sun without squinting my eyes!"

Only yesterday he had been sitting with a group of animals who were talking about how they always had to scowl when they tried to gaze at the Sun. Owl told them his grandmother had told him when they scowled like that the Sun thought they were making faces at him. "That's why sometimes he gets so mad and hot," Owl explained, "and he nearly burns us up. And

other times he goes off and hides and we nearly freeze."

Rabbit felt neither hot nor cold, but just right. As he watched the huge orange-red ball getting nearer the earth—his ground home, the animals had named it—he thought the Sun beamed on him warmly. Shafts of golden light touched the glistening white of a puffy cloud and the mountain was the hue of burnished copper.

"I don't feel lonely any more. That's such a friendly color," Rabbit thought. And when he had thought some more, he raised his head proudly and said, "Why, I guess the Sun is trying to tell me he's a friend of mine because I didn't make a face at him."

He smiled cordially and waved a paw in greeting. Then he put his front paws around his mouth and shouted skyward, "I'm pleased to have made your acquaintance."

"And I'm pleased to have met you at last," a harsh voice cut in sharply behind him.

Rabbit's skin tingled as if the words had gone through him like knives. He turned about quickly. A mass of daggers seemed to be growing out of the ground in front of him. There sat the giant Flint in the grass.

A shiver crept along Rabbit's spine and he wished it would not for he was greatly embarrassed. From his ears to his tail his fur rose up, and Rabbit was powerless to smooth it down. He wondered whether Flint had noticed. Then his legs began to act up. They wanted to run him away, but Rabbit pressed them hard into the ground, hoping they would stay until he could think of something to say. He was a very good talker which often helped him over difficulties. Something to say? He searched his head, found nothing and could think of nothing. And there went another one of those awful shivers down his back. Rabbit said to himself, "Well, let it go down; maybe it'll drop off at the end of my tail." But not that shiver. It turned around and started right back toward Rabbit's head, as if it were running on a single track railroad.

Rabbit had something to say.

"C-c-c-old up h-h-here," he stammered, giving himself a good shake and trying to appear chilled.

The giant burst out laughing. "Cold!" he jeered. "I'm not fooled. You're scared. I think you're a coward." Then he began to sing, "Rabbit's a coward, Rabbit's a cow-ward, a cow-ward, a cow-ward!"

Rabbit flushed angrily, but smiled sweetly, just as if he loved Flint's song and thought it excellent music. This was no time to quarrel with a giant. He shot a quick glance at his back. Yes, the hair was standing straight up. Nobody could be deceived; Rabbit was scared. But he hoped he would not run away. He shot a quick glance at his legs. Three of them were off the ground. Rabbit set them down firmly and gritted his teeth.

The giant's song halted abruptly and a black look came into the singer's face.

"Why, oh why, oh why, oh why?" he asked, pounding the earth with a powerful fist.

"What's he going to do now?" Rabbit wondered and permitted the three legs once more to relax.

"Why, oh why, oh why, oh why?" repeated Flint.

Rabbit's bright eyes traveled rapidly over the landscape. They were picking out the safest place for him to run to.

"Why did I speak to you when I did?" Flint asked with an extra hard whack of his fist, and Rabbit winced, but the giant didn't seem to mind the blow. "Tell me why?"

His voice broke as tears glazed his eyes. Rabbit was clever enough to realize that this was the moment for him to say just the proper thing to make Flint want to be a little friendly. Rabbit said entirely the wrong thing.

"You spoke to me because you're very neighborly," he said ingratiatingly.

"Neighborly!" exploded the giant. "Neighborly! Never! I'm getting old and soft-hearted. That's the trouble. I had no business speaking when I did. In another second you'd have bumped up against me. Right now you should be running down this mountain yelling with pain." The giant wagged his head sadly. "Just old and soft-hearted."

And from this Rabbit took his cue and said the proper thing. "I can't believe you're soft-hearted," he said with truth and boldness. "The animals say you have the hardest heart of—of—well, of anybody!"

Flint's eyes sparkled with delight. "Do they say *that?*" he asked, and was quite willing to believe "they" did say *that*. "Tell me, what else do they say?"

Well, Rabbit was a good talker and here was his chance. "They say," he said, "you're the cruelest, fiercest, wildest, meanest, hard-heartedest, most impossible, terriblest, wickedest giant in the world!"

Flint pondered these slurs pleasantly. "Now, that's really very nice," he said. "I didn't know the animals thought so badly of me."

Rabbit was catching his breath after uttering all those big words. But he hadn't caught much when he saw the joy passing from Flint's face and grief taking its place.

"It's just too bad I spoke," the giant said sorrowfully. "You're such a clever little animal, I'd like to have heard you yell. You've probably got a very distinctive yell."

"Perhaps I'll get hurt yet and you'll hear me yell," said Rabbit consolingly.

Flint's face brightened again. "Do you think you really will?" he asked eagerly.

"Perhaps," Rabbit said, and this sounded almost like a promise.

"Good," Flint said. Then he added, "Rabbit, you don't realize how lucky you are not to be suffering right this minute."

As soon as he uttered the word "lucky" Rabbit's shivers ceased. Rabbit liked being lucky. With luck everything always went much better for him and, looking over the enormous figure of the giant, he realized he would need all the luck there was to send him out of Atagahi. For no reason at all, except because Rabbit was clever, a plan that looked good enough to drive Flint from the mountain capered through his head. The thought said, "A fellow that big enjoys eating."

In his friendliest manner, Rabbit said, "You're the lucky one, Flint. I was just about to get my supper. I never like to eat alone and so I'll pick up something for you. Would you like to have supper with me?"

Flint was too astonished to speak. No one ever before had offered him supper for, after all, feeding a giant is a large undertaking. Even Flint had complained of this.

"Why—er—uh—er——" the giant stammered.

"Why—er—uh, g-g-go ahead and p-p-prepare my dinner. I'm sure I don't mind."

Rabbit turned to hide the satisfied expression in his face. "I'm going to look for food," he called over his shoulder as he began running down the mountain, "and I'll be right back."

"Don't hurry," said Flint, settling himself to wait comfortably. "And don't run like that. You might hurt yourself. Be careful of the rocks too. Bear a little to the right. There are none there."

Rabbit snickered but replied soberly, "I'll be careful, Flint, just for your sake."

Off in the bushes where Flint could not see him, Rabbit stopped running and sat down. Rolling over on his back he folded his forearms under his head and crossed one leg loosely over the other. His free foot began to swing up and down briskly and rhythmically. This was Rabbit's favorite position for thinking.

"'Be careful, you might hurt yourself,'" he mimicked Flint. "Ugh! What an ugly giant! But I'll fix him. I wonder if I could really scatter him to the winds."

For a long while Rabbit wondered. Then his foot swung faster. He seemed satisfactorily absorbed in thought.

Afterward he stood up spryly and headed for the

woods. It was dusk when he returned to Flint with his arms laden with appetizing grasses and bundles of leaves. He piled these up and went off for more.

"I'll fill up Flint until he's ready to pop," he declared, bustling among the green snake-grass.

On his two last trips he brought in twigs and dead tree branches for a fire. Flint watched all these preparations hungrily. He thought Rabbit should have moved faster, but he did not say a word, lest conversation delay the supper. To hasten the meal he generously provided the spark to light the fire. Rabbit rolled the greens into balls and set them to bake in the hot ashes. While they cooked he started scooping out a burrow in the ground a little way from where the giant sat.

"What are you doing?" Flint asked.

"Making a place to sleep," said Rabbit. "I get drowsy after supper and can't keep my eyes open. I was born in a hole and must sleep in one. A draft on my back always starts a cold."

Rabbit looked slyly at Flint. The giant appeared to be in a fairly amiable mood and so he asked, "Flint, do you go to sleep after you eat?"

"You bet I do," the giant replied robustly. "Next to eating I like sleeping best."

Rabbit poked his head into his burrow and frantically began shoveling dirt. Flint's reply had made him so happy that he was afraid he would shout with joy, and he would not have liked Flint to know he felt just that way.

When the tunnel was three times his length, Rabbit came out and joggled the dust from his fur coat.

"Say, isn't it time to eat?" Flint inquired impatiently.

"I'm going to serve supper right away." Rabbit took a long pointed stick and rolled the steaming balls from the ashes toward Flint, who began eating them greedily, apparently not minding that they were hot. Rabbit nibbled a few mouthfuls. He was much too excited to eat. Besides, in spite of all his talk about sleeping, it was the last thing he really wished to do.

Supper was soon over because Flint gobbled up everything so fast. As he licked the taste of the last green ball from his mouth, he remarked, "That was a delicious meal." But, of course, it never occurred to him to say, "Thank you." Then he began to yawn. Rabbit had never heard such awful yawns. They were far worse than Puma's which had ruined Rabbit's speech at the council.

Throwing more wood on the fire, Rabbit picked up a sturdy stick which he had dragged in with the firewood and sat down opposite the giant. As soon as

Flint closed his mouth and could hear, he said casually, "I love to whittle. Too bad I haven't a knife."

"I thought you were going to sleep," Flint said.

"Oh, I am, but first I want to give my dinner time to digest or I'll have bad dreams."

"Hah! Hah! Hah!" laughed Flint. "Bad dreams! I love 'em. I'd like to dream one bad enough to make me wake up. But there isn't any. Hah! Hah! Hah!"

Rabbit didn't think this funny, but to be agreeable he laughed. And this made Flint laugh again, and so Rabbit was obliged to laugh a little more. He was thankful when another yawn interrupted the giant's mirth. After this, with a clatter of his points, Flint dropped back on the grass. He was going to sleep.

"Flint," said Rabbit, "I think I could use one of your points for whittling. Will you give me one?"

The giant sleepily broke off a small piece of his suit and tossed it to Rabbit. There was another spell of yawning and Rabbit thought this surely ought to carry Flint to slumberland. But it didn't. Flint began to murmur. Rabbit cautiously crept closer to hear.

"The supper was delicious," the giant was mumbling, "but what if he had stumbled over me? I might have enjoyed that more. He's a smart fellow. Probably got an unusual yell. I'd like to hear it. Gosh! Now, which would I like better? The supper or the yell?"

A yawn that sounded like a storm breaking over the mountain halted these thoughts. It gave Rabbit a fright and he jumped to a safer distance where he sat stiffly on guard, ready to flee. But Flint quieted down and after a long wait Rabbit was convinced that any well-fed giant ought to be sleeping. With jerky, measured leaps, he quietly moved toward Flint's head. Halfway there he heard that same mumbling. "The supper or the yell? The supper or the yell? Dearie me, I wish I could make up my mind! I'd like to know which would have pleased me more. It was an excellent supper, and he didn't eat much of it. Um-mmm! Oh, well, he'll get hurt anyway. He promised. Now, that's fine. I'll have both supper and yell."

At last, his mind was at peace and Flint could drop off to sleep, and he wasted little time about it. Snores began to pour from his lips. Disgusting sounds they might have been, but to Rabbit, waiting with thumping heart, they were exquisite music. His mind at ease, he resumed his seat before the fire and his whittling. Far into the night he whittled and he wasn't quiet about it either because he wanted to make sure the giant was a sound sleeper. Flint really was and not once did he even turn over.

When Rabbit put down his stick it had a point as

cruel looking and as sharp as any on Flint's costume. With the knife-like piece that the giant had given him, Rabbit dashed off into the darkness and some time later came back with a stone crudely shaped like a hammer. He had chipped the rock himself. And Flint still slumbered on, his snores rumbling and echoing over the mountain.

Rabbit laid his stone hammer beside the sleeper and picked up his stick. With all his might he jabbed the pointed end into the middle of Flint. The giant stirred and his snores stopped. Rabbit hastily grabbed his hammer and began pounding the stick, as if it were a nail, deeper and deeper into Flint. He drove it right through him and into the earth. This woke up Flint, but too late. Rabbit had pinned him to the side of the mountain.

Dropping the hammer Rabbit rushed into his hole. From the safety of the entrance he observed the giant trying to free himself. Rabbit prayed that the stick should hold. Flint wriggled and writhed, pulling from side to side, and banged himself against the mountain. With each bang, some of his points broke off and, like pebbles, rolled down the mountain. Their clatter and *bumps* kept Rabbit busy jumping into the depths of his burrow, and his ears, nose and legs and the hair on his back were wildly warning him of danger, but he stayed on bravely, now and again peeking circumspectly and quaking lest his stick should give way.

He speculated on Flint's fate, surmising that when the Sun came out next day the giant, without his clothes to protect him, would start withering and eventually dry up like the cobs of corn the animals sunned and put away for the winter. "I'll see the Sun in the morning," Rabbit said, "and, of course, now that we're friendly he'll probably oblige me by cooking up Flint in a hurry."

Flint, however, was never cooked. When he could not free himself, he got terrifically mad. He strained and puffed until he looked as though he were ready to burst. And, with all that food packed into him, that is just was he did eventually. Rabbit heard a terrible C-R-R-RACK!!!! and ran as far back in his burrow as he could and wished that he had dug it much, much longer. When he had the courage to creep back to the opening, there was no giant outside, but pieces of Flint seemed to be dropping from the sky in all directions. A fragment struck Rabbit across the nose and he darted back into his hole and stayed there the rest of the night, very nervous and very jumpy.

As day was breaking he stole to the entrance. All was calm and the bulging figure of the giant was nowhere in sight. But as far as Rabbit could see, pieces of Flint were scattered over the mountain. And so Rabbit walked bravely from the hole, took a deep breath, stood up straight and strutted about, triumphantly examining the wreckage.

Flint was destroyed beyond a doubt and no more would he harass the animals of Atagahi. Rabbit was a little disappointed that the giant had blown up. He would have liked to lead some of the animals up the mountain to see him baking in the Sun. And that reminded Rabbit; he looked up to say, "Good morning," to the Sun. But it was so bright, he squinted and suddenly he felt exceedingly warm.

"Oh, well," said Rabbit, "the Sun is probably mad at one of the animals who's making a face. I'll speak to him later."

Rabbit had not eaten a really good meal since the day before, so he began to nibble himself some breakfast hurriedly. He was eager to get down below and tell his friends what had happened. He chewed grass and pictured the welcome the animals would give him.

"Gee, I'm a hero now," he told himself proudly.

Rabbit thought the animals probably would hold a feast in his honor and he could almost see himself sitting importantly by the side of Black Bear and listening, as modestly as he could, while the leader of the animals made a speech praising him. Over this idyllic scene splattered a dark blot and the vision vanished. Rabbit frowned and in alarm raised a paw to his nose. Then he looked at the paw. It was smeared with blood.

"Cabbages and lettuce leaves!" he cried. "My nose is split. My face is ruined! I won't look like much of a hero with a split nose. Oh, my!"

And the little hero began to cry. When he could stop, he carefully wiped the nose a piece of Flint had cut and decided to stay on the mountain for another day and night and wait for his wound to heal. Besides, Rabbit was very tired after his adventures. He did not wait for his breakfast to digest, but crawled wearily into his burrow and went to sleep.

Rabbit's nose never grew together again. At least that's a story from Atagahi and the Indians say it is why all rabbits have split noses. And about the giant Flint, that's another of the stories. Rabbit having scattered him, the Indians say this explains why flint, a hard substance out of which men made tools and weapons before they discovered iron, is found in many parts of the world.

Chapter IV

THE FIRST FIRE . . . . .

The animals gave Rabbit a beautiful party and everybody had a lovely time honoring the hero. But the festivities were over and done with now, and Rabbit had made a lot of new friends and everyone still spoke of how brave he had been and praised and thanked him. Besides, the big animals went out of their way to speak to him these days in the woods, and of course all of Atagahi wanted to see his split nose. Rabbit, therefore, was rather pleased with his wound and he was very patient about exhibiting it and always told exactly how he was wounded.

So life in the happy land of contented animals pursued its smooth way once more. Rabbit and Terrapin were again taking their long walks and this exercise had not changed in the slightest degree. Terrapin swept along behind Rabbit breathlessly trying to keep up with a pace much too fast for him. As always he was winded and needed to rest and he didn't have an idea in his head how to make Rabbit rest. If Terrapin said simply, "I'm tired," then Rabbit would say with disgust, "Oh, you're so slow, Terrapin," and Terrapin was sick of being called slow and so he would not give up and say, "I'm tired."

This was his predicament one Tuesday morning as he panted along behind Rabbit. How could he get Rabbit to rest without appearing himself to need the rest?

"I can't say, 'Isn't that a beautiful view?'" Terrapin argued silently. "Rabbit knows that old trick of mine. And I can't say, 'Look at this bug,' or 'Have you seen this tree?' That's all been used before."

With his last breath Terrapin did have to resort to an old subterfuge. "Look there, Rabbit," he said, "at that pine tree. Do you know about it?"

Annoyed, Rabbit said, "Tch, tch," and added, as Terrapin could have predicted he would add: "You're so slow. Always wanting to rest. I've told you about that pine tree dozens of times."

"I know you have, but I'm tired," said Terrapin, drooping and dull. "Tell me about the tree again, Rabbit. It's the most refreshing story I know, only I don't know it exactly. I forget parts." And with a sigh of relief he settled his upside-down-saucer-like body on the ground and let all four feet dangle.

Rabbit curled his fluffy tail around his feet and folded himself comfortably over it. "When plants, animals and flyers," he began the story, "were first put on the earth they were told to stay awake for seven nights. All of them were able to keep their eyes open the first night, but the second night some dropped off to sleep. My dear friend Puma"—yes, indeed, they were great friends since the destruction of Flint—"stayed awake and when he goes about at night, he has the power to see just as if the Sun were shining. Owl also kept awake and there were a few others. Some of the trees never went to sleep—like the pine over there, and the cedar, spruce, holly and laurel. And so they keep green summer and winter."

Terrapin sighed wistfully. "My grandparents must have gone to sleep," he said.

"They were probably the first to close their eyes," said Rabbit. "Why, you even sleep during the day."

Terrapin's legs sank to the earth lifting his shell, and again he rushed after Rabbit. It wasn't long before this speed had him gasping and looking for a good excuse to stop. Rabbit, however, himself paused.

"I know this place," he said, looking at a tall tree. "Raven lives here. Let's call on him."

With the scanty breath he had, Terrapin shouted, "Ra-a-a-a-a-ven!"

Rabbit looked at him, puzzled and frowning. "Whatever's the matter with you?" he asked crossly.

"Nothing, oh, nothing at all," said Terrapin.

"Then why're you shouting?"

Terrapin blinked and looked surprised. "I'm calling on Raven. You said——"

"Tch, tch, tch," said Rabbit which meant that Terrapin was very stupid.

"You said——" Terrapin began defensively.

"Be quiet," Rabbit interrupted. "You don't have to explain. I know just what you're thinking."

"I'm thinking what is it you're thinking I'm thinking," said Terrapin and choked.

Rabbit thumped his back and his coughing stopped. "Now be quiet and watch me," said Rabbit. "I'm going to show you how to go calling."

Picking up a small stone Rabbit knocked it against the tree. With a fluttering of wings Raven appeared on a branch overhead. "Good morning, Raven," Rabbit said. "Are you at home to visitors? Terrapin and I are calling."

"I'll be right down," said Raven in a sad voice. He circled overhead and dropped onto the grass by his callers. "I'm pleased to see you. This is a surprise, although I thought I heard Terrapin's voice before you knocked."

"Oh, yes, you did. I was calling," Terrapin bragged, which made Rabbit fling out his forepaws in a gesture of despair. "Humph!" he groaned. "You'll never learn anything."

Raven was perplexed, but really did not care to know what these two were talking about. He began to complain politely, "If I had known you were coming, I would have had some acorns for refreshments."

"Ooooo!" exclaimed Terrapin appetizingly. "Rabbit, let's go and then come back. Then Raven'll know we're coming and we'll get acorns."

Rabbit gave him an ugly, disapproving frown, and Terrapin, not to see it, pulled his head into his shell. Inside he pondered. Why was Rabbit displeased? He thought of the usual ways in which he displeased Rabbit, but none applied here. Of course, Rabbit was his best friend and was always telling him things for his own good. That was it, Terrapin concluded, Rabbit was trying to say something for his own good. He probably was not really displeased and so with this thought in his head, Terrapin slid the little knob back into the open.

"I've always admired your shiny black feathers," Rabbit was saying to Raven.

"I think I would rather be a white bird," said Raven dismally. "I should have been white, if it hadn't been for my great-great-great-grandfather who was bent on being a hero."

"Ooooo!" said Terrapin. "Like Rabbit—he's a hero."

"No, he wasn't like Rabbit," said Raven gloomily. "He was a bird."

"I don't believe I've heard of your ancestor," said Rabbit. "What did he do?"

"Nothing but change the color of our feathers. And that wasn't what he set out to do. It happened accidently because he was just stupid. I call him a half-wit, since half-way he was all right."

"What did he do?" Rabbit repeated.

"My great-great-great-grandfather was big and strong and a long-distance flyer," said Raven mournfully. "He was among the first flyers in Atagahi. There wasn't any fire to keep them and the animals warm and the Lightning, in that careless way she has of tearing everywhere, thoughtlessly dropped the fire in a tree on a far-away island. My great-great-great-grandfather because he was strong was the first to volunteer to fly over the water and bring the fire to the animals."

"Very brave of him," commented Rabbit authoritatively.

"Very brave," echoed Terrapin, as if he were an authority too.

"No, just rash," Raven lamented. "He flew across the water and lighted on the tree on the island. Then, for the first time, it occurred to him that he needed something to carry the fire in. And there he perched in the tree for the longest time wondering what he should do. Meanwhile, the heat from the fire was scorching his beautiful white feathers black. When my great-great-great-grandfather noticed that he became panicky and flew back without the fire. And we've all been black ever since. The idiot!"

"Who finally brought us the fire?" Rabbit asked.

"Alas, that's not my family story," Raven deplored.

"Even so, your family has an interesting story," said Rabbit, trying to cheer up the gloomy bird.

The First Fire

"I liked it," said Terrapin, adding his word of cheer.

But Raven remained despondent and fretted and complained and very soon Rabbit and Terrapin said, "Good-by," and went on their way through the woods.

"Rabbit!" called Terrapin, breathless of course. "You forgot to tell Raven when we'd call again. He'll want to know and have acorns for us."

For the life of him, Terrapin never could figure out why Rabbit stopped still for an extra long rest right then. He hadn't said, "Look at this bug or this tree," but somewhere there was a trick concealed in what he had said, for Rabbit sat down and Terrapin sat down and nothing was said about his always being slow. Naturally, Rabbit did talk to him, but it was all about politeness and refreshments and he told Terrapin while it was very nice to be offered food when calling, still he must never have his host believing he had called simply because he expected to be given acorns. When Rabbit had said all this, which took a long time, he stood up to resume the walk.

"Ummm!" said Terrapin with appreciation. "That was a grand rest," and remembered it had something to do with acorns. The next time he grew tired he must remember to mention acorns. Apparently they could deceive Rabbit into stopping.

Their next halt was by another tall tree.

"This is Woodpecker's house," said Rabbit. "Let's call on him." As he stepped toward the tree, a prickly burr tangled itself in his long tail. "Cabbages and lettuce leaves!" exclaimed Rabbit. "Look at that burr."

He picked up his tail and was loosening the burr when he heard a *knock, knock, knock!* Rabbit looked up and saw Terrapin bumping his hard shell against the tree's trunk.

"Terrapin!" Rabbit was aghast. "Stop that racket. What are you doing?"

"Calling on Woodpecker," said Terrapin. "See—like this," and again his shell knocked the tree.

"Stop!" shouted Rabbit, running to the tree and pulling Terrapin away. "You'll insult Woodpecker with that noise. He'll think you're making fun of his knocking a tree the way he does."

Terrapin looked confused and his head wobbled as if the burden it carried were too heavy. "But, Rabbit," he protested, "at Raven's you said——"

"But, Terrapin, this is Woodpecker's," explained Rabbit.

Terrapin gazed wide-eyed at his surroundings, noting them for the first time. "Yes, that's true, that's true," he said, sagely nodding his head.

Rabbit whistled for Woodpecker. There was no answer because Woodpecker was not at home and so

The First Fire

Terrapin and Rabbit walked on. They next came upon a hooting owl sleeping in a tree.

"Sh-h-h-h-h!" whispered Rabbit. "Look at the big white circles around his eyes."

Terrapin studied the sleeping bird and said, "If I stayed up all night I'd get dark circles under my eyes."

Presently they came to a small pond.

"Water Spider lives here," said Rabbit. "Let's sit down and wait for her."

"She's an awful gadabout," said Terrapin. "I've never yet found her at home when I swim over to see her."

In the clear water they saw a catfish swimming by.

"Hi!" shouted Terrapin, but the fish went ahead without returning the greeting. "Catfish are sort of stupid," he commented. "I don't care much about them. Do you know why their heads are flat, Rabbit?"

"I'm an animal, not a fish," said Rabbit with dignity. "I know little about things in the water."

"You wouldn't care about catfish even if you knew the water," said Terrapin. "They say moose trampled on their heads when they came to the River to drink. The catfish were too lazy to get out of the way."

"That's a silly story," said Rabbit. "I don't think much of fish anyway, and I don't care at all about water."

"Oooo!" said Terrapin, "I like water for swimming. You'd love swimming, Rabbit, if you tried it once."

"No, I wouldn't. And I'm tired of sitting here by the water waiting for Water Spider. Come on, let's go."

Terrapin pointed a front foot up the pond. "Here

comes Water Spider now," he said. "Look! Ooooo! Hasn't she got speed!"

Rabbit looked and saw a fluffy black ball sliding over the top of the pond. It moved very fast, zipping from side to side, seemingly without a notion of where it wished to go. As it came nearer he saw the bright red stripe that circled Water Spider's fuzzy body. He was about to call, "Hello," when *zut!* she darted out of sight. Far off on the pond she reappeared and then, at breakneck speed, she slid to the bank where her callers were waiting.

"Hello!"

"Hello!"

"Hello!"

"Do you swim?" asked Terrapin.

Water Spider gurgled, which was her way of laughing. "No, I skim and without a splash."

"Really!" Terrapin was amazed. "I always splash getting into the water."

"You don't need to. Look!" Water Spider dove under the water. She was up in a flash. A tiny bubble of water clung to the hairs of one leg. She flicked it off and smiled triumphantly up at Terrapin. "See," she said. "I'm not even damp and there wasn't a splash, was there?"

Terrapin was dumb with admiration.

Rabbit was bored with all this talk of water and he took advantage of the silence to change the subject. "You've a nice spot here, Water Spider," he said.

"It's convenient, just a step from the water," said Water Spider.

There was the loathsome water again. Rabbit hastily introduced another topic. "Do you happen to know who brought the fire to the animals?" he asked.

"Of course I do," said Water Spider. "It was my great-great-great-grandmother."

"Did she!" exclaimed Terrapin. "How nice! Was she a half-wit?"

"Terrapin!" Rabbit reproved.

"Certainly not!" said Water Spider indignantly.

Terrapin stared and wondered what he had done wrong.

"Your great-great-great-grandmother must have been very smart," said Rabbit tactfully. "Raven failed to bring the fire back. How did she do it?"

"Black Snake and several of the owls failed too," Water Spider asserted proudly. "They didn't have anything to carry the fire in, but before my grandmother crossed the water she spun a web the shape of a bowl and fastened it onto her back. It was simple enough for her to reach the island, but once there her troubles began. The way to the tree where the fire was led through tall grass and blades of grass cut the threads holding the bowl to her back. Again and again she had to stop and tie up the bowl. But my grandmother was smart. As she went along she pushed back the grass and made a path to return by.

"When she got to the tree with the fire she shook a small burning coal into her bowl and then sped back over her path and across the water—*like this!*"

Before Rabbit knew what was happening, Water Spider had shot over the pond and returned.

"Giminee!" she gurgled. "I bet my grandmother didn't go any faster than I did that trip."

"Ooooo!" said Terrapin. "It was so fast I didn't see you. But then I had to go and blink my eyes once."

"I'll do it again, if you keep your eyes open," said Water Spider obligingly.

"All right," said Terrapin and the next second was exclaiming, "Marvelous!" because Water Spider already had returned.

Rabbit was not interested in Water Spider's antics. "These water animals," he said to himself with disgust, "are all skittish. They can't keep their minds on one thing. Terrapin's just like that. The sight of a little water upsets him and he forgets everything except the water. I wish Water Spider would settle down and finish the story about her grandmother."

But there went Water Spider skimming over the pond again. She was now showing Terrapin a new turn and leap she was practicing. Terrapin was entranced. It all looked very silly to Rabbit.

Water Spider skated back to her callers.

"How did your grandmother keep the fire from burning up the bowl?" Rabbit prodded.

"I've just been showing you," said Water Spider. "Like this." And she was racing over the pond once more.

"Marvelous!" applauded Terrapin.

Rabbit was puzzled. "I don't understand," he said.

Water Spider looked at Terrapin and gurgled. "These land animals!" she said. "They just never understand anything about water." And she turned around a couple of times gurgling, and Terrapin giggled.

"It was this way, Rabbit," said Water Spider and away she raced.

"Marvelous!" Terrapin repeated.

Rabbit was annoyed. "But I still don't understand, Water Spider," he said. "Please sit down and tell me."

Water Spider gurgled and said, "You've forgotten, Rabbit, I never sit down. But anyway, I'll tell you. It was like this. My great-great-great-grandmother scuttled across the water so quickly that she ran faster than the coal could burn her web. The animals were waiting for her on the shore and they gave her a big welcome—after setting the coal on an immense pile of wood they had collected. And that's how the animals have had fire ever since."

"You could have done that too," said Terrapin. "No fire could burn as fast as you run."

"I don't believe it could either," Water Spider admitted. "Look!" And there she went.

Rabbit was thoughtful. "Wouldn't it be dreadful without fire?" he observed.

"I'd miss it," said Terrapin. "I like heat."

"Fire doesn't mean a thing to me one way or another," said Water Spider. "My grandmother really had no use for it. I don't think she went near fire afterward. Look!" And off she skipped.

Terrapin kept his eyes open and watched her. "And to think she never gets her feet wet," he said admiringly. "You know, Rabbit, that's really very extraordinary."

Rabbit was unimpressed. "Water Spider's far too nervous," he criticized. "I think all this running is bad for her."

Water Spider was back. "I forgot to say good-by. Good-by." And she was gone.

Terrapin gaped after her in surprise. When he

could see the little figure no longer, his face screwed up and he began to think.

"I'll never, never understand about calling," he said dully. "Here we are the visitors and yet Water Spider is the one who says she's going. I thought we'd say we're going and then after that she could go. This seems backward to me."

"Oh, it's all right," Rabbit assured him. "Terrapin, this is Water Spider's."

Terrapin glanced around. "Yes, that's true, that's true," he said, nodding his head understandingly.

Chapter V

RABBIT AND POSSUM LOSE THEIR TAILS . . . .

BEING a hero made Rabbit, after a while, very vain. He got pompous too, and strutted through the woods with his chest stuck out, talking loudly to attract attention, and talking too much, as his best friend Terrapin could not help but notice. Terrapin was not finding him such a good companion any more.

"What's got into Rabbit?" he asked Ground Squirrel. "He seems to have lost his head completely."

As usual, Terrapin was wrong. What Rabbit actually lost, because of his vanity, was his beautiful long tail. One day he was bereft of it, and seven days later Possum parted with his for practically the same reason.

Fate began to weave her web around Rabbit one afternoon when the first breath of winter chilled the air. The animals were thus warned of the cold months ahead, and so most of them gathered in a warm, sunny spot, took off their fur coats and began putting them in shape for freezing weather. They shook them out and they licked them and combed them with their claws and everyone was looking handsomer for his industry.

The heat of summer always made Brown Bear so lazy and for weeks on end he simply didn't bother to take care of his fur. Naturally he was amazed to see how really attractive his coat was after he had washed and smoothed it down and removed tangled lumps of caked mud. He stood off a little way to get a better view of his cleaning.

"Oh, my, I do like my coat," he said admiringly. "In the sunlight it shines like gold."

"I like my coat too and I don't need the sun to make it shine like gold," boasted Red Fox.

"Neither of you has a coat to compare with Black Bear's," snarled Wolf who was rarely agreeable. "His is the color of the night and I wish I had it for prowling."

"Poof!" said Puma. "I prefer my coat. It's a good color, warm, doesn't show the dirt, and my hair isn't so long that it's always in a tangle."

"I like my coat," said Deer modestly.

And then a dozen animals were all talking at once and saying they thought their coats were best. Black Bear nodded to Bullfrog.

Rabbit and Possum Lose Their Tails 67

"C-C-C-R-R-ROAK!" honked the Marshal and the noise subsided.

"There's no sense to this argument," said Black Bear. "If we have to declare whose coat is the finest, we'll call a council to decide. Is everybody here?"

"Otter isn't," said Raven. "I saw him far up that way the other day when I was flying around. He has the prettiest fur I've ever seen."

"Otter has a lovely coat," said Black Bear.

"Yes," agreed Puma. "I think it is the finest."

One after another, as the animals remembered Otter, they acknowledged his fur was more beautiful than theirs. Rabbit alone took no part in the discussion. He had a nice coat, he thought, and soon after Brown Bear started the argument, he began washing and brushing his fur in anticipation of the moment when one of the animals would point to him and say, "Why, there's Rabbit, our hero. Look at his coat. It's the prettiest!" And then everyone, recalling Flint, would proclaim Rabbit's coat the finest.

This was the sort of thing that had been happening to Rabbit ever since he became a hero. Wherever he went he received all the attention, he was given gifts, and he was called the cleverest and the handsomest and the bravest and heaps more *ests*, which delighted him very much and made him want to be always in the midst of his friends so that he could hear their compliments.

But Rabbit waited and waited, scrubbing and brushing, and no one noticed his coat. Instead, on every side, he heard Otter's praises sung, and Rabbit was envious.

"Someone will have to find Otter and bring him to the council before we can decide," Black Bear said. "Who'll go look for him?"

"I will," Rabbit quickly volunteered, for the idea suddenly ran through his head that perhaps, if he were able somehow to keep Otter away from the meeting, his coat would be voted the finest.

Rabbit traveled four days in the direction Raven had last seen Otter. He was a hard little animal to find because he had various homes. Rabbit had never seen Otter, but when he came upon him at last, he recognized him. Everything the animals had said about his coat was true. The fur was the most beautiful Rabbit had ever seen. From behind a tree, Rabbit regarded it with mounting envy as he watched the owner scurrying about gathering wood and making a fire. Then and there Rabbit resolved not only to keep Otter from the council, but to have his lovely coat.

"Good afternoon, Otter, I'm Rabbit," said Rabbit stepping away from his hiding-place.

Rabbit and Possum Lose Their Tails 69

"Why, how d'ye do," said Otter cordially. "I've always wanted to meet you. Where are you going?"

"The council sent me for you," said Rabbit, and purposely did not mention anything about coats.

"It's nice of you to come so far to find me," said

Otter. "We'll have some supper and sleep in my house tonight and start out in the morning."

Otter served a delicious supper because he is an exceptional hunter and collects so many sorts of food, and besides he is an agreeable companion. Rabbit liked him immediately. One of the first things he did was to ask Rabbit to tell about Flint and he listened with great interest to the story, interrupting from time to time with squeals of delight, "Oh, how splendid!" and of admiration, "Oh, how brave!" Rabbit thought he had never met a better listener, and there were moments when the idea of taking the coat bothered him a little. He would have liked to keep Otter for a friend. Of course, after he took his coat, he would not want to meet him again.

Rabbit lay awake all night thinking and seeing the handsome coat as it had glistened in the firelight. That was an unforgettable sight, and by morning Rabbit had figured out a plan for his theft.

He helped Otter fix breakfast and afterward the two set out for the council. In the middle of the afternoon, Rabbit began picking up twigs which he tied into a bundle and carried on his back.

"What's the wood for?" Otter asked.

"It's for a fire so we'll be warm tonight," said Rabbit.

"I'll gather some too," said Otter obligingly.

And Rabbit had a twinge of conscience because Otter was such a kindly, helpful animal and already trusted him like an old friend. But there was that beautiful coat for which he was justly famous. Rabbit's conscience deserted him and he determined to take the coat and forget friendship.

At sunset they camped beneath a tree near the bank

of the River. Rabbit knew the spot well and had chosen it purposely. He made a fire and with Otter's help cooked some supper. After they had eaten, Otter, who was tired from the long day of traveling, stretched out before the fire to sleep. Rabbit gazed up at the night and his tongue clucked disappointedly, "Tch, tch, tch."

"What's the matter, Rabbit?" Otter asked, sitting up.

"I've picked a bad place to camp," said Rabbit. "This is called The-Place-Where-It-Rains-Fire, and I remember the sunset was very red tonight. That's a bad sign. Perhaps we'll have a rain of fire tonight."

"Shall we move our camp?" said Otter.

Rabbit considered. "No, I think not," he decided. "It's very late and too dark. You go to sleep and I'll keep watch. If it rains fire we're near the River and you can run down and jump in. Better hang your coat on a limb under the tree so that the fire won't touch it."

Obediently Otter took off his coat and hitched it onto a limb. He went to sleep thinking how kind Rabbit was to stay awake and protect him.

Rabbit kept the fire going and when Otter was asleep went off into the woods. He came back with a wide piece of wood that looked like a paddle. He waited for the fire to die down to red ashes and then he scooped these up and flung them high into the air. As they drifted in the soft breeze, he shouted:

"Otter, Otter! Wake up! It's raining fire!"

Otter rubbed his eyes drowsily. They opened a little way and glimpsed sparks fluttering overhead.

"Run for the water!" cried Rabbit.

Trustingly Otter ran to the River and dove in. As soon as he heard him splashing in the water, Rabbit reached for the beautiful coat and disappeared with it into the night.

After three days Rabbit neared the Chopped Oak and he put on Otter's coat. The animals were watching for him and when they saw him in the distance, they shouted, "Here comes Otter! Otter is coming!"

One of the smaller animals came down the path to greet Rabbit, whom they mistook for Otter, and escort him to the best seat at the meeting. As he passed through the council Rabbit heard the admiring "Ohs!" and "Ahs!" of his friends over Otter's beautiful coat. Rabbit was delighted, for once again he was the center of attention. Of course, his friends believed they were exclaiming over Otter, but Rabbit thought that in time he could make everything all right for himself and it would be forgotten that the coat ever had been Otter's. But right now Rabbit kept his paw over his face and his head down so that he would not be recognized. He fooled all the animals except wise old Black Bear who found "Otter's" behavior most unusual.

"What is the matter with Otter?" he asked Brown Bear.

"I'm astonished," said Brown Bear. "I've never seen him so bashful."

"He's always friendly and walks into the council meeting calling, 'Hello,' to everybody," said Black Bear. "His manners are generally the best. I've never known him to behave disrespectfully and keep his paw before his face. I think I'll investigate."

Black Bear shuffled over to where Rabbit was seated. "Are you ill, Otter?" he asked.

Rabbit shook his head, "No."

"Then why've you got your paw in front of your face?" said Black Bear. "Put it down."

Rabbit wished he had made the shake of his head say "Yes," for he did want to keep his face hidden.

"*Take away your paw!*" commanded Black Bear sternly.

But Rabbit couldn't obey. He rose from his seat and started to run off. Black Bear reached after him and caught his tail. Rabbit tried to yank himself free, but Black Bear had a good hold. Forgetting about his face, Rabbit lowered his paw and gripped his tail, tugging with all his might.

"Why, it's not Otter!" the surprised council exclaimed. "It's Rabbit!"

Black Bear growled. "Shame on you, Rabbit," he scolded. "You'll have to be punished for this trick."

He gave Rabbit's fluffy tail an extra hard jerk—*and pulled it out!*

And this is how, the Indians say, rabbits came by their stumpy little tails. Since that time otters live mostly in the water, although when they're young they do not take to it as naturally as ducks. The mothers have a difficult time teaching their babies to swim. And since they are going to spend most of their time in water, they must learn to eat fish. Baby otters never care for fish at first and their mothers scold them and insist they eat it. "It's good for you; it'll help you to grow," the mothers probably tell them. By the time otters are grown, they love fish. In the water they are shy animals and do not give their friendship so trustingly as when their ancestors lived only on the dry land.

The council was very angry with Rabbit for his deception. The animals said he ought not to be allowed to take around the invitations to the farewell dance of the summer. Rabbit enjoyed this mission because it gave him an opportunity to visit and talk with everybody, and in this way he picked up lots of gossip which pleased him and was useful in entertaining friends.

Black Bear, however, said he believed Rabbit had had enough punishment in losing his tail and besides nobody delivered the dance invitations quite so well as Rabbit. Black Bear also said he had had a long talk with Rabbit who had repented his conduct.

"I'll never steal Otter's coat again," Rabbit had promised.

Black Bear scratched his ear and looked unhappy. "No, Rabbit, you won't steal Otter's coat again, but you'll find some other mischief to get into," he said. "You're always causing some sort of trouble in Atagahi. And yet you can be very good. I wish you were good all the time. I have a lot of work to do and I get awfully tired when I have to scold and punish. It's a big job leading the animals and I can't do it well if you keep me all worn out with your badness."

Rabbit felt ashamed of himself and hung his head.

"Forgive me, Black Bear," he said. "You can just sit back and rest now. I'm going to be good."

Black Bear smiled down at the contrite little animal and patted his head. "I know you mean well, Rabbit," he said, "and that counts a lot with me."

When Rabbit started out Terrapin followed him.

"Terrapin, you can't go with me," said Rabbit.

"Please, I've always wanted to deliver dance invitations," Terrapin begged.

"Don't be silly," said Rabbit. "I've got to get around in a hurry." Terrapin looked sad and his eyes grew watery and so Rabbit said, "I'll tell you what. Day after tomorrow, I'll deliver my last invitation to Possum's. Meet me there. If you begin crawling now, you'll just about make it."

Terrapin did not quite make it. Rabbit came upon him the day after tomorrow still some distance from Possum's, resting in the path and sniffing the air distastefully.

"What's that nasty smell?" Terrapin asked.

Rabbit took a deep breath. "Ugh!" he said in disgust. "That's Mink. He's related to Skunk. Let's hide until he passes. I don't want to meet him. If I do, I'll have to invite him to the dance. The council doesn't want him there either. He's a thief."

They stepped out of the path and hid behind a tree stump.

"What does Mink steal?" Terrapin whispered.

"Everything," Rabbit whispered back. "A long time ago he stole something important and the council decided to throw him into fire for punishment. But when the animals smelled him roasting, they thought they had been too cruel and so they dragged him out of the fire. Ever since he's smelled like he smells now—like burned meat. When he gets excited, or when he fights or steals, he smells worse. Mink didn't learn a thing from his roasting. He's probably stealing something right this minute; that's why he smells so awful."

Sure enough in a moment Mink rushed over the path carrying a large mouthful of something or other. In another moment Wolf dashed by in pursuit.

"Phew!" said Terrapin, blowing out his breath. "What an odor! Rabbit, I'm glad you didn't get burned for stealing Otter's coat." Terrapin chuckled. "I'd never follow you again if you smelled like Mink."

Rabbit said nothing and neither did he chuckle along with Terrapin. He wanted to forget about Otter's coat. "I'm not a thief like Mink," he said to himself indignantly.

They found Possum sitting outside his house and combing his tail in the sun. He accepted the dance invitation lazily and then said loftily:

"I'll come if you'll arrange to give me a special seat. With my beautiful tail I ought to sit where everyone can see it. And, of course, I don't care about mixing with the crowd. It would never do. They'd crush my lovely tail, even step on it, I bet. They're so careless, those animals, but then they've never had an exquisite tail to look after."

Rabbit thought Possum very conceited and would have liked to tell him so, but instead he said politely, "The council wants everyone to be comfortable and if you insist on a special seat you shall have it."

"I do insist," said Possum emphatically. "Perhaps I'd better have two seats. I'll put my tail on one. It's really too beautiful to lay on the filthy ground."

"I don't know if we can spare you two seats," said Rabbit. "The dances are always crowded."

"Well, I know that," said Possum, "but I really must have two seats. After all I shall be the only animal there with an exquisite tail. I should think you would be honored making arrangements for it. You don't often have the chance."

Rabbit nearly bit off his tongue holding back the words he most wanted to say to Possum. At that he almost said, "Shucks!" and walked away. With an effort, he stayed and replied calmly, "We'll do our best to see that you enjoy the dance, Possum."

"That's what I expect," said Possum haughtily, and Rabbit and Terrapin hurried off.

"The nerve of that little beast!" Rabbit fumed when they were out of earshot. "Two seats! And he can't mix with the crowd! Well, he ought to be told the animals don't care about mixing with him, he is such a snob. He's done nothing all his life but take care of that tail. And it's not such a wonderful tail. Mine was better."

"Maybe Black Bear'll pull out Possum's tail," said Terrapin.

"I'd prefer pulling it out myself," said Rabbit. "Every year when I come here with his invitation he's alway's sitting in the sun and combing his tail and he always wants something better than anyone else has at the dance. Possum makes me sick!"

Just then a small, clear, singing voice at Rabbit's feet said, "Chur-r-rk, chur-r-rk."

"Why, hello, Cricket," said Rabbit and Terrapin. "How's business these days?"

"Only fair," said Cricket. "My barber shop isn't crowded as it is in the springtime. This time of year the animals let their hair grow for winter. Most of the day and evening my assistants and I sit by our fire and sing just for our own pleasure. Too bad there's seldom anyone to listen. We've got some new songs and our quartet sings them beautifully. Only we do like listeners. I don't understand why our singing doesn't attract customers even if winter is coming on."

"I know where you can get a customer," said Rabbit.

"Where?" asked Cricket eagerly.

"We've just left Possum. He'll want a lot of fixing up for the farewell dance."

The eager expression went out of Cricket's face. "Oh, Possum," he said without enthusiasm. "He's already my best customer, but we don't enjoy working for him. He never listens to our singing. All he thinks about is that bushy tail of his. My barbers would trim him up better if, just once in a while, he encouraged them by requesting a song."

"Isn't he tiresome with that old tail?" said Rabbit.

"That old tail of his," said Terrapin disdainfully.

Cricket snickered. "You know, I've often thought," he said, "what a good joke it would be on Possum to shave his tail. I've been tempted many times when I'm trimming it and Possum's sitting up in my chair so grandly."

"Why don't you?" urged Rabbit.

"Why don't you?" urged Terrapin.

"Well, we always try to please our customers," said Cricket. "If I shaved Possum's tail, he wouldn't be pleased."

"But you'd be pleasing the rest of your customers," argued Rabbit.

"I'd be a pleased customer," said Terrapin whose shell had never been known to sprout one hair and so he had no need of a barber.

"You should consider the majority of your customers and not just one," Rabbit persisted. "I bet if you shaved Possum's tail you'd have a better business.

Why, the animals would flock to your barber shop to hear how you did it."

"Don't you think any would come to hear the quartet?" Cricket asked wistfully.

"Oh, certainly," said Rabbit. "And perhaps once they hear it they'll want to come back oftener. Besides, Cricket, I believe you would actually be doing Possum a good turn. He hasn't a friend in Atagahi because of that tail. If he lost his fine tail, he wouldn't be so selfish and he'd have more time to make friends."

"Yes, that might happen," Cricket agreed, "but what would Black Bear say? I wouldn't want him to be angry with me."

"He pulled out Rabbit's tail so he must think it's the right thing to do," said Terrapin.

"I think Black Bear will be glad to have Possum's tail shaved," said Rabbit. "He's got a lot of work to do and scolding the animals wears him out. Now you know Possum needs a terrible scolding. Black Bear'll have a rest and won't get tired if you punish Possum for him."

"I'd like to do something for Black Bear," said Cricket. "All right, I'll shave Possum's tail."

For a long time the three of them sat around like conspirators and discussed the tail-shaving. Cricket said he would not have much trouble managing and he could fix it so that Possum would not know his bushy tail was gone until he began dancing tomorrow night. This would permit all the animals to participate in the fun when Possum found out.

"This is what I'll do," Cricket explained. "First, I'll comb out his tail. That always makes Possum so comfortable and lazy that he takes a little nap. When he's getting ready for a special occasion like the dance, I usually wind a red string about his tail from one end to the other to keep the hair in place. Now all I have to do is to go around and around that tail between the loops of string and snip the hairs at their roots. Possum won't know what I've done until tomorrow night when he begins to unwind the string during his dance."

The next evening Possum, in his most superior manner, pranced into the dance on two hind legs, gingerly carrying his tail, wound with red string, high in front of him where it could not touch the filthy ground. Rabbit met him at the entrance to the dance circle, where he had been waiting anxiously, and with a relieved glance observed the red string. Thus far anyway, it appeared Cricket had been able to carry out his plan.

"Good-evening, Possum, we're glad to welcome you to the dance," said Rabbit.

"Show me to my special seats," Possum ordered discourteously.

His rudeness in nowise upset Rabbit whose face had a beautiful smile on it when he replied agreeably, "Certainly, come right this way."

Possum was hardly seated when Marshal Bullfrog announced that it was his turn to dance. The vain little animal swept gracefully to the middle of the dance circle, carefully laid down his tail behind him and, holding the end of the red string tightly in one forepaw, signaled with an imperious wave of the other paw for the music to commence.

> *"See my beautiful tail,*
> *All bow down and hail."*

Thus sang Possum as he spun around unwinding the red string.

Howls of glee rose from the circle of animals. Possum mistook them for admiring cheers. He danced faster.

> *"See what a fine color it has,*
> *The envy of all beasts, alas!"*

The clamor grew louder. " 'The envy of all beasts,' " the animals repeated, laughing as if to burst their sides. Possum was a trifle disconcerted but still believed his dance was being tumultuously approved. He whirled confidently on his toes.

> *"See how it sweeps the ground*
> *As I go round and round."*

The audience roared. Brown Bear was unable to

control his laughter. His ribs began to ache and he rolled helplessly into the middle of the dance circle.

"Haw! Haw! Haw!" he guffawed. " 'It sweeps the ground.' Look at the ground! Haw! Haw! Haw! It needs sweeping now!"

With an irritated stamp of his feet, Possum stopped dancing. Everyone was laughing and pointing to the ground. He lowered his eyes. The ground was littered with the dark, bushy hairs of his tail which, save for a soft down, was bare to the skin. Possum was overcome. He slumped to the ground, rolled over and began to cry.

That is why, according to the Indians, possums to this day have smooth tails. If you speak to one, he'll roll over, just as Possum did that night, and sometimes a curious grin appears on his face. He isn't grinning; he's grieving for the lost hairs of his tail. And when he cries like this the tears drip from his mouth. You see, Possum had been so selfish and so hard-hearted all his life, that he wasn't able to cry like the other animals whose tears stream from their eyes.

If a possum doesn't grin and cry when you notice him, you can expect he'll play as if he's dead. "Playing possum," you've heard people call it. Possum himself started this trick right after he returned home from the dance. He was troubled by visitors who wanted to look at his smooth tail. Possum didn't care to talk to anyone and least of all did he wish to exhibit his sorry-looking tail. So he'd just roll over and pretend he was dead until the callers went away.

Cricket had a lot of visitors too, but he didn't play possum. He heartily welcomed them all and his quartet sang to them, and the barber shop did a flourishing trade even though winter was near.

Chapter VI

Tournament Day

A week after the dance the animals gathered in the clearing at the Chopped Oak for Tournament Day, the last and most exciting event held to say good-by to summer. During the morning the slow-moving animals played a ball game against the fowls, or slower flying birds, and in the afternoon the fastest runners contended against the fastest flyers. Terrapin was on the morning team and Rabbit played in the afternoon.

Rising before dawn Terrapin ambled off to the tall grass where he plaited himself a necklace. Everybody dressed up specially for Tournament Day. Each year Terrapin slung a grass necklace around his throat, although he always promised that next year he would positively appear with a different decoration. But he never did because, even if his small head had unexpectedly presented him with a new idea, when it came to "dressing up" Terrapin was handicapped.

"What shall I do for a decoration?" he began asking himself several days before the games. "I'd like to wear a costume. A grass skirt? No, that'd never do; there's not enough room between me and the ground. A belt? I haven't any waist-line; a belt would slip. Bracelets? My arms are too short. If there were only some way to make flowers stick to me somewhere. A hat? I haven't the head for a hat."

Even the grass necklace was a failure, once the ball game began. On the first occasion the ball was thrown directly at him, Terrapin's head instinctively ducked to safety within his shell and the necklace, left high and dry with nothing to hang onto, slipped off.

And so here comes Terrapin on Tournament Day crawling onto the ball field gaily "dressed up" with his familiar necklace. But the spectators gave him a cheer and a compliment, even if they had been led to expect a different costume this year.

"Hooray for Terrapin! Isn't he handsome in that necklace!"

Terrapin bowed, acknowledged their cheering and looked ever so pleased. He pushed out his neck longer, to show off his necklace and to appear, if possible, a little handsomer. Holding this pose he marched stiffly over to Captain Alligator and reported his arrival.

Alligator was deep in an argument with Bat.

"Please let me play on your team," Bat entreated.

"I can't," said Alligator. "You're not an animal."

"Then what am I?" asked Bat desperately. "The fowls say I'm not a bird. I've got teeth and so I must be an animal."

"You're so small, you must be a bird," said Alligator.

Half-jumping and half-flying, Bat made his way dejectedly to a place among the spectators, leaving a curious little animal, resembling a cross between a squirrel and a mouse, to plead with Alligator.

"Please let me play," implored the curious animal.

"What are you?" Alligator asked impatiently.

"I think I'm an animal," said the funny little thing, "and I'm sure I could help you to win."

Alligator laughed. "A mite like you!" he scoffed. "You'd just get in the way."

The whatever-he-was walked dispiritedly to where Bat was seated and gloomily took the place next to him.

Marshal Bullfrog rolled out a long "C-R-R-ROAK!" signaling the fowls and slow runners to get ready for the ball game. Three minutes later he croaked again. Black Bear tossed out the ball and the tournament began.

The game was played somewhat like football. There were goal posts at either end of the field and the players scrambled to get hold of the ball. If the animals got it, they tried to carry it over the fowls' goal for a point. If the birds got it, they flew down the field toward the animals' goal.

Terrapin played the game backward and it was quite all right that he did. He was a goal guard. He took his place near the animals' goal posts and, when the ball rolled near him, he backed up to it and a hind leg jerkily kicked it toward the birds' goal.

"Bravo, Terrapin!" the spectators shouted with relief, for they had held their breath all the while Terrapin was slowly backing. Nobody was ever certain Terrapin's foot would not miss its mark. Often it did.

But, on another play when the ball almost bounced on Terrapin's head, he slid into his shell, and the game was nearly lost then and there, and the watchers hissed and booed his clumsy and none-too-courageous playing which almost gave the fowls a score. Fortunately, Alligator recovered the ball in the nick of time and with a sweep of his powerful tail shot it to the center of the field. Within his shell Terrapin never heard a boo or a hiss. After a prudent wait, his head reappeared. His face was serene, for all the time he had been shut away Terrapin had been congratulating himself on his playing. After all he had acted quickly and saved himself a good bump which might have upset him.

"We want a goal! We want a goal!" the spectators yelled.

As if to oblige them Alligator caught the ball firmly between his teeth and started toward the fowls' goal. His teammates formed a ring around him and fought off the bird players. The fowls set up an awful chattering as they flew and fluttered trying to break through the animals' defense, but they did not get near Alligator nor could they hold back the circle advancing closer and closer toward their goal.

"Hurry, Alligator, hurry!" howled the animals' friends among the spectators, and these were mostly the larger animal players.

"Get that ball! Get that ball!" the fowls' friends, the fast flyers, screeched frantically.

But the animals were stronger than the fowls and they hung onto the ball. Some of the smaller birds flew into the circle and reached Alligator, but their fragile beaks and spindly legs could not pry open his powerful jaws. And so it seemed likely the fowls were on the verge of losing another ball game. They had never won one, but that did not appear to discourage them. Every year they came back and fought bravely until they were defeated.

Alligator's circle was now within a few feet of the goal. There was one minute more to play. Suddenly Captain Bald Eagle rose from the midst of the struggling teams and flapped skyward. He soared higher and higher until he disappeared above a small cloud.

"Where's he going?" the fowls' friends wondered.

"He's leaving in disgust!" jeered a friend of the animals, and his friends laughed. The fowls' friends looked sad and downcast.

But Bald Eagle unexpectedly swooped, passing through the small cloud, and dropped heavily on Alligator's nose.

"*Ouch!*" screamed Alligator, opening his mouth and losing his grip on the ball.

Startled by his scream, his team turned to him in dismay, forgetting the ball game and forgetting also to keep their places in the circle. The ball rolled on the ground, and Turkey, quick as a flash, poked his long neck through a gap in the broken circle, picked up the ball and raced off to the animals' goal. He threw the ball between the posts just as Marshal Bullfrog croaked the game was over. The fowls had won their first ball play.

In a second the sky was black with birds, twittering and cackling with joy over the victory. Those that didn't fly much, or not at all, clustered around Turkey on the ground, congratulating him and patting him on the back with their wings. Black Bear strode onto the field, perched Eagle on his shoulder and led the victorious fowls in a parade around the field.

"You played a beautiful game," Black Bear told Bald Eagle who was ruffling and shaking his dark feathers. Some of the small cloud through which he had swooped still clung to them.

"Well, we did our best," said Terrapin to Captain Alligator.

"Uh-huh," agreed Alligator unenthusiastically as he rubbed his sore nose. There was a dent where Eagle landed, and what's more the dent stayed there ever afterward. Even the alligators of today have the self-same dents on their noses.

After lunch Captain Brown Bear summoned his fast-running animal team for a talk.

"We must win the ball game this afternoon," he said. "The fowls won this morning. We can't disgrace the animals by letting the birds have another victory."

As he finished speaking Bat hobbled up and asked for a place on the team.

"Why, you can't play with us," growled Brown Bear. "You're too small."

"But I run fast and I'd help win," said Bat.

"You'd just be a little nuisance," said Brown Bear. "You'd probably get stepped on. No, I don't want you on my team."

Crestfallen Bat slunk away and right after him came the funny little nameless thing begging to play.

Brown Bear laughed at the sight of him. "Ho! Ho! Ho! You on my team. Ho! Ho! Ho! Don't you know this is the best ball team in Atagahi? And you want to play on it! Ho! Ho! Ho! Next thing I know I'll have an ant crawling out here and asking to play."

"I'm bigger than an ant and I can run very fast," said the little thing.

"You're not much bigger than an ant and I don't know whether you can run," said Brown Bear. "But I do know you're not an animal and I can't put you on my team. My advice to you is to keep off this field before someone walks all over you."

The bear turned away and went busily ahead with preparations for the game. The whatever-it-was hopped off behind Bat.

"Are you certain you did right turning down those players?" Black Bear asked Captain Brown Bear.

"You're not going to have an easy time this afternoon. The birds are so happy over the fowls' victory, they're going to give you a stiff battle. I think you'll need all the help you can get."

"Listen, Black Bear, those two little mites wouldn't be any help," said Brown Bear. "They'd be in our way. And don't you worry about us not winning. The big animals haven't lost a ball play yet. I don't care how excited the birds are. They're not the ball players we are."

"You seem pretty certain of yourself, Brown Bear."

The captain of the animals smiled. "Sure, I'm sure," he said confidently. "My team will walk away with the game."

Black Bear shrugged his shoulders. "We shall see."

Meantime Bat and his queer companion made their way to Captain Eagle who, because of his wonderful playing that morning, had been invited to join the fast-flying team.

"Please let us play," begged Bat.

"I can't," said Bald Eagle. "Both of you have four feet. That makes you animals."

"The animals say we aren't animals," said Bat.

"Then put them on our team," suggested Martin. "We want all the players we can get. We want to win."

Captain Eagle could not quite make up his mind to consent.

"Please," pleaded Bat.

"Please," squeaked the funny little thing.

Bald Eagle's head wagged doubtfully. "But you can't fly," he objected.

"We could take some of the wing-patch and cut them wings," suggested Hawk.

"Still they might not fly," said Eagle.

"We can make the wings and try them anyway," said Martin.

"I think perhaps they would fly," said Hawk.

"All right, go ahead," Eagle yielded. "Anything to win. You'll have to hurry though. It's almost time for the game."

Hawk flew off and came back with the wing-patch. A couple of birds with sharp beaks cut a pair of wings from it and Hawk stretched them over two small frames of fine twigs which meanwhile he had been attaching to Bat's legs. He gave the wings a final pat into place and said, "Now, Bat, try them. See if they'll fly."

Bat flapped his new wings and they shakily lifted him onto the lowest branch of the nearest tree. "Wheee!" he shrieked excitedly. "I can fly! Wheee! Here I go," and he took off, less shakily, for a higher branch.

Bald Eagle threw him a ball which he caught easily, although flying, and furthermore he held onto it. Most of the birds could catch while on the wing, but afterward the ball always slipped from their beaks. Unlike Bat they had no teeth with which to grip.

Bat's little wingless comrade sat forlornly on the ground and, sad-eyed, watched the ball practice. He was wondering where he was going to get wings. Practically all the wing-patch, except a few scraps, had been used on Bat.

When Hawk was satisfied that he had turned out a real flyer, he tripped over to the unhappy little thing, and hopped about him several times studying his figure.

"Hummm," Hawk meditated. "Maybe we can fix you up. You've got too much skin around your hind legs. I believe we could stretch it as far as your front legs and then you'll have something like a pair of wings."

"Will it hurt?" the funny little thing asked anxiously.

"A little, perhaps, but you shouldn't mind that if I give you wings," said Hawk.

"Oh, I won't mind, if I know ahead of time. I'll be expecting the hurt."

Eagle held onto one side of the little whatever-he-was and Hawk went to work on his other side, pulling and stretching the skin until he had a strip long enough to reach from the hind leg to the front leg. When he had it securely in place, it looked like a furry ruffle. Eagle changed sides with him and Hawk put a ruffle between the other legs. It must have hurt pretty badly, all this skin pulling because Hawk, when he took his eyes off his work, saw the queer little near-bird holding his lips tightly together, as if he were keeping back a scream or a groan. But he didn't even wince, not once. Hawk patted his small back approvingly and said:

"There you are, old sport. See if those wings are any good to you."

"Old sport" ran up a tree and then he sailed through the air, landing in another tree. Then back he flew to the first tree. And how quickly he could run up and down the branches! No bird had his speed running.

"He looks pretty good," said Captain Eagle.

Hawk's eyes followed his leaping-flying creation. "He looks a lot like Squirrel," he observed. "I think we should name him Flying Squirrel."

And so, at last, the whatever-he-was had a name. From that moment he was Flying Squirrel.

Marshal Frog's signal rolled across the field and the players hurried to their places. The second croak sounded and Black Bear threw the ball into the center of the field.

With a bound Flying Squirrel, who was so happy he could not keep still, was on the ball. He dug his teeth into it and sped for the trees along the side of the field. He caught onto an overhanging branch and then springing, running and flying he passed to other trees in the direction of the animals' goal.

"Don't let him over the goal line," shouted Brown Bear who could hardly believe his eyes.

"He'll not pass us," answered the guards.

But Flying Squirrel did pass them. He leaped over their heads and dropped the ball behind them and the goal line, scoring a point for the birds.

The spectators broke into wild cheers. They had never seen such a thrilling play. It was most unusual because the birds rarely ever scored against the animals. Twittering and chirping the flyers sailed joyfully into the air. Captain Eagle had a time getting them to come back to earth and go on with the game. He had a time with himself for that matter because he was so happy his wings were begging him to soar. But he remembered he was the captain and he stayed below, and he fluttered his feathers because some of that small cloud obstinately clung to them.

As for the animal players they stood off in a group without anything to say.

"Now watch yourselves this time," Brown Bear cautioned them. "Of course we'll win the game. We always do, but keep your eye on Flying Squirrel. Don't let him get the ball again."

When Black Bear threw out the ball the second time, Flying Squirrel did not attempt to go after it. There would have been no use because every animal player was watching him. That was why, with nobody watching him, Bat was able to pounce on the ball, hold it and fly right down the field, over the guards' heads and score before Brown Bear's team had time to figure out where the ball was. When they knew, it was too late.

"Now tighten up this time," Brown Bear lectured his players. "Look out for Flying Squirrel and Bat. Remember, you're stronger than those birds. Don't let them score again. Of course, we'll win. The fast flyers have never yet won."

"They seem to be winning now," said Rabbit.

"The game has just begun," said Brown Bear. "We'll hit our stride soon, but it'll be better if you don't let the flyers score any more."

That, however, was something the animals were unable to prevent. Flying Squirrel and Bat were too quick on their feet and wings for them, and besides they had teeth. Rabbit, for all his cleverness, could not think up a single trick to stop them. And so, when Marshal Frog croaked his last croak, the score was six to one in favor of the birds. Only the swift deer had managed to get a goal for the animals.

The birds were jubilant over their victory and filled the air with their happy songs. They had won both ball plays on Tournament Day! It was almost unbelievable because they had never before won as much as one game.

The animal players walked gravely off the field, and there weren't any cheers for them. Brown Bear followed them in a daze. He couldn't understand how his team had been defeated, but Black Bear talked to him sometime later and explained.

"I think you were over-confident," said the leader of the animals. "It's not good to win all the time. This defeat will open the animals' eyes to their weaknesses and next year you'll play harder to win."

Brown Bear had not given a thought to next year, but there was an encouraging idea. Next year he'd show the birds! Just then the victorious birds flew low overhead, escorting in triumph Flying Squirrel and Bat. Black Bear smiled and waved to them.

"Too bad you turned those two down," he remarked to Brown Bear.

The captain nodded agreement. "I'll put them on my team next year," he said.

"It's too late now," said Black Bear. "Flying Squirrel and Bat are forever lost to the animals. Henceforth they belong with the flyers."

That night, winners and losers sat down to a feast around a big fire that took the chill off the frosty air. It was a gay party, and the birds had a merry time twitting the animals over their defeat. Flying Squirrel, Bat, Captain Eagle, Turkey, Hawk who had made the wings, and Martin who had insisted that Flying Squirrel and Bat play, huddled together happily, saying little because they were rather weary after the ball game and all the congratulating and back slapping. Captain Brown Bear also had little to say, but every time his eyes lighted on the little group his head nodded sadly. Flying Squirrel and Bat were birds henceforth and he was to blame. Ah, well, next year, and he hoped some funny little crawling thing would ask to play on his team. He'd welcome him all right.

At a late hour the celebration ended and the winning flyers gathered up their presents to start for their homes. Gifts from the losers to the victors were the custom after the ball play and the animals had given each flyer a gourd filled with food.

"I'm flying South early tomorrow," said Martin. "I'll leave my gourd in the Chopped Oak until I come back in the spring." (Which he did, and the following spring he made his nest in the gourd. Out West where the Indians live now, they hang out gourds every spring for the martins to nest in.)

Before saying, "Good night" and flying away to Pilot Knob, Captain Eagle gave his wings a good shaking. Bits of the cloud still stuck to his feathers. And he never did succeed in getting rid of all of them which is why, the Indians tell us, the feathers of the bald eagle are flecked with white.

Chapter VII

THE CRAWFISH AND THE GREAT BUZZARD . . . .

There were no lively times in Atagahi during the winter. The birds flew away to the South, and some of the animals thought the cold months so unworthwhile that they curled up and slept through them. Those that remained awake kept to their burrows, or whatever shelter they had, crouching over their paws to protect them from frostbite. Only Wolf, Deer, Fox and Possum never had to worry about being frostbitten as they walked through the snow and over the ice, but in spite of this privilege they were lonely and longed for the spring when their friends could walk with them.

So, since no one seems to be enjoying the winter, let's make this particular one very, very brief and end it with this paragraph.

That brings us to next spring, when the travelers are returning from the South and Rabbit is spending more and more hours each day outside his burrow. His legs are feeling frisky, his nose is tickled by a confusion of scents from newly sprouted greens, and ideas and plans fill his head.

Terrapin is near by, but somewhat cross. For him, spring lags a trifle. The swimming in the River is still chilly, and unbearably so way down deep. For a week Terrapin has been trying to touch bottom, but the icy water turns him back and sends him shivering to the sunny bank. Terrapin is always irritable and never himself in the spring until the sand of the River's bottom has tickled his toes.

"Terrapin," said Rabbit one evening, "before the leaves are thick on the trees, let's climb the mountain and look at the valley."

"I don't like climbing," objected Terrapin. "Don't you want to see the valley?"

Terrapin's small face wrinkled peevishly. "I've never seen a valley and so how would I know whether I want to see one?" he demanded.

With an anxious frown Rabbit studied his cranky little friend. Of course, he realized Terrapin was not feeling well on account of spring, but he had never known him to be in such a state before, and he had known him many springs. Rabbit thought Terrapin did look rather pale and decided he needed the trip up the mountain, if only to take his mind off his troubles over touching bottom. Why anyone should get sick because he could not swim down deep in the River, Rabbit did not pretend to understand. Certainly he never felt that way about water, but terrapins and fish were queer in this respect.

"Well," said Rabbit, "I want to see the valley and I'm going up the mountain tomorrow morning." He expected, in fact he planned, that this announcement should make Terrapin, who always wanted to go everywhere with him, say he would come along. But Terrapin sat moodily silent with an unbecoming, dissatisfied expression on his face, and so Rabbit had to think up another scheme to lure him on the expedition.

After a while he said, "You know, Terrapin, I think this river is too deep."

"You'd think any river too deep," snapped Terrapin.

"No, I'm thinking about you. Now, if you dove into a shallower stream, you'd get to the bottom quicker."

Terrapin blinked and poised his head pensively. He'd never thought of that, but he said stubbornly, "Oh, I don't know."

"At the foot of the mountain the Stream is shallow," said Rabbit. "You can see the bottom. I should think you'd go over there and dive in."

"That Mountain Stream!" exclaimed Terrapin in disgust. "It's too swift. I don't like water that rushes. I might get carried right into the Haunted Whirlpools. It's not safe."

"But I know where there's a quiet stretch and the Stream doesn't move any faster than the River," said Rabbit.

"Do you?" asked Terrapin with interest, and then seemed to regret his burst of enthusiasm, for he added sullenly, "Aw, but there's no sand there."

"Yes there is," Rabbit hastened to assure him. "There's sand and a few rocks."

"Hah!" Terrapin sneered. "I knew something was wrong. I don't like rocks. They bump."

"They don't bump unless you bump into them," Rabbit pointed out. "After all, you move; the rocks don't move."

Again Terrapin's head was poised thoughtfully. What Rabbit said was true, he had to admit, but rocks always angered him when they bumped. And if he tried kicking back at them, it hurt and sometimes took the skin off his toes. But to touch bottom! Ecstatically Terrapin sucked a deep breath through his mouth as if he were already tasting the delight of this thrill. Then he put back the scowl on his face. Something inside of him still made him want to act grumpy.

"All right, I'll go and try the Stream in the morning," he said with no great amount of interest.

They set out the next morning early when the moon was still up, but as they approached the mountain the Sun began his climb up into the sky vault. Rabbit's quiet water in reality was a long narrow pond which backed away from the racing Mountain Stream, forming a trough which seemed to mark the dividing line where the lowlands ended and the mountains started to grow. It frequently overflowed and so the earth on either side was perpetually damp, almost swampy, and reedy grass flourished there, particularly on the lowland bank. Rabbit had pushed his way through the tall grass and was waiting for Terrapin when he noticed a curious sight on the soft, wet shore. Innumerable small mounds with holes running down their centers rose up like towers out of the mud.

"Terrapin, what are these?" Rabbit asked.

With an effort Terrapin brushed aside the wide reeds obstructing his path and joined Rabbit. "Oh, those," he said. "They're crawfish houses."

"Houses!" said Rabbit. "Goodness me, what a muddy damp place to live."

"I guess crawfish are glad to have them like that," said Terrapin.

"Phew! Imagine living in such a hovel! I couldn't."

"You would, if you had a warm red shell," explained Terrapin. "A long time ago, you know, the Sun scorched the crawfish. That was when he was first hung in the sky vault too close to the earth. Afterward the Sun was set higher in the sky. If he hadn't been I guess the rest of us would have been cooked red."

Rabbit peered down the crawfish holes. "I don't see how crawfish were scorched if they lived underground," he remarked.

"They didn't have houses like these in those days," Terrapin went on. "This was in the beginning when everything was covered with water and the land was down below. The fish were happy enough, but the animals weren't. They asked the fish to swim down and bring them up some land to stand on, so their feet could get dry. The fish tried willingly, but they couldn't bring up any earth. Finally the crawfish went down. They had a good idea of what to do. They piled up the muddy bottom in mounds just like these houses, except there weren't any holes in them. They came afterward."

Terrapin crawled to the edge of the pond and testily dipped in a leg. "Ummmm!" he exclaimed with more joy than he had shown since the coming of spring. A second leg sampled the water, and he said pleasantly, I'll touch bottom today all right."

With a frown of annoyance Rabbit watched Terrapin dabbling in the water. He waited impatiently for the end of the story about the crawfish. These water animals! Skittish they were, and never kept to anything long; always hopping about and swimming. Such was Rabbit's unspoken criticism. He waited, squirming and fidgeting and "ahem-ing," but saw no indication that Terrapin remembered there was a conclusion to his tale, and so Rabbit prodded, "How long afterward?"

Terrapin stared vacantly at Rabbit. "I'm sure I don't know," he said.

"Terrapin, you must have some idea."

"Oh yes, I have. Today I'm going to touch bottom."

"I don't mean that," said Rabbit in exasperation. "I mean the crawfish. Finish up about them. When did they put holes in their houses?"

"Right afterward," continued Terrapin as if there had been no interruption. "When the crawfish got the land above water they made the mistake of standing on it. They're fish and should have stayed in the water. Then the Sun came along and scorched them and so they dug holes in the middle of the mud they had brought up and crawled down inside to cool off."

Rabbit pursed his lips and looked doubtful. "Whoever told you such a story?" he asked.

"I've heard it often from the crawfish," said Terrapin. "It's their story and they're quite proud of it."

"A likely tale," Rabbit commented scornfully. "I don't believe a word of it."

With terror in his eyes Terrapin glanced backward at the collection of mud towers. "Shhhhh!" he warned.

But the warning came too late. Rabbit had spoken in a loud voice and he had been heard. Small red heads with popping, angry eyes and long trailing whiskers shot out of the holes. Over each head brandished two pairs of claws, snapping open and shut in a most menacing way. From their mud houses emerged an army of angry crawfish and advanced boldly on Rabbit.

"*Plop!*" spoke the pond as Terrapin, who knew how crawfish could pinch, dove in, heading rapidly for the bottom.

"*Swish!*" said the air above the pond as Rabbit, utterly frightened by the unfamiliar sight of a crawfish army, leaped the narrow stream and sped up the mountain.

When he stopped running Rabbit had climbed quite high. He turned and looked back, not exactly sure that he wouldn't find the crawfish at his heels, although he had sniffed and twirled his ears before actually coming to a standstill.

Relieved of his pursuers Rabbit sat on his haunches and gazed downward over the tops of the trees, still almost bare of leaves. Nothing blocked his view and so for the first time Rabbit saw the valley far below him. Mountains enclosed it, their crests rising and dipping irregularly so that Rabbit thought they looked for all the world like a collection of gigantic upturned faces. There were round ones, with cheeks blown out, and there were sharp ones and thin ones, and Rabbit chuckled over one with a nose tipped roguishly at the sky.

In the valley itself he could see the lines of trails he had traveled all his life. They appeared so different way up here. He recognized one particular path. It curved and almost formed a half-circle, and Rabbit always had believed this path to be absolutely straight.

There was the pond at the foot of the mountain where he had escaped from the crawfish. It seemed so much narrower, as if one could actually straddle it, and Rabbit, when he was forced to leave, had thought it so wide and wondered whether he could make the jump without getting wet. Rabbit's eyes found the exact spot where he had jumped, but they did not catch a glimpse of Terrapin.

A flapping of wings overhead drew Rabbit's attention from the valley. He looked up and saw Buzzard dropping toward him.

"Hello, Rabbit," said Buzzard, landing with a bounce and folding his wings. "What brings you way up here?"

"Hello, Buzzard. I came up to look at the valley before the leaves cover the trees."

Buzzard himself looked solemnly at the scene below. He was not a merry bird, but serious, dignified and probably not as old as he looked. "It's a pretty sight," he mused. "I always make a high flight just about this time of the year to get a good look at the valley. That's where I'm bound today."

"Why, I shouldn't think you'd be that interested in the view," said Rabbit. "You're flying over the valley all the year round."

"I don't see much of it once the leaves are out," said Buzzard. "But I really make the flight to honor my ancestor the Great Buzzard who made this valley."

"Did the Great Buzzard really make the valley?" asked Rabbit inquisitively.

"Yes, and the lakes and even the mountains," said Buzzard. "It was a long time ago when the earth had just been brought up from the bottom of the water."

Rabbit's ears perked up attentively. This was the second time today he was hearing that the land came up from underneath the water. He looked at Buzzard speculatively. What sort of tall tale was he ready to relate? "Anyway," said Rabbit to himself, "he has a reputation for honesty and he isn't skittish." So Rabbit inquired, "Was the earth brought up from under the water—really?"

Buzzard nodded his head and said, "Yes. Don't you know that story?"

"I've heard it," said Rabbit and looked around to see whether there might be a crawfish about before he added, "but I can't say that I believe it!"

"It's a true story, Rabbit."

Rabbit scratched his head reflectively, but he was unconvinced. "I don't know," he said, "it's hard for me to believe it. I guess I don't understand fish. Anyway, Buzzard, tell me about the valley and how your ancestor made it."

Buzzard cleared his throat with a cough and gravely began.

"The earth was wet and muddy and the animals were crowded onto one small dry spot. The birds felt sorry for them and everyday one flew off a great distance seeking more dry land. But there was no other place. One morning the Great Buzzard flapped into the sky and he was determined not to return until he had discovered a nice roomy meadow. He was the strongest bird, but even so he flew and flew without finding the meadow and he was so tired he barely had the strength to flap his wings. They drooped lower and lower and pretty soon he felt them bumping the ground ever so often. The Great Buzzard was too weary to raise himself higher and so he just went sailing along as best he could and letting his big, powerful wings smack the earth.

"Then he couldn't fly any more. He told himself he had to give up and land even if he sank wing-deep in the mud. Great Buzzard landed, but what was his surprise to find himself perched on the side of a mountain, just like this one—maybe it was Blood Mountain—and the ground underfoot dry. He was looking down into a valley, like the one below us. Where his wings had hit the slushy mud, they had dipped into it and made valleys. Where they struck it awfully hard, they made deeper hollows and the water ran into them and became lakes. The lakes had drained off the water and that's how the land was dried. Where the Great Buzzard's wings hadn't touched at all hills and high mountains were standing."

Buzzard ended his story and Rabbit looked incredulously at the large and spacious world before him. He liked the story, but—— "Ridiculous!" he was saying to himself. "No buzzard could have done that. It's as absurd as the tale about the crawfish."

This time, however, Rabbit was careful not to announce his disbelief. He did not care to have an army of angry buzzards after him. Vainly he sought something nice and tactful to say, but nothing came into his mind. Naturally his silence told of his doubts.

"You question my story, don't you, Rabbit?" Buzzard asked.

Rabbit stared helplessly at the bird and tried to summon words to his lips. "Well, er—er—a—ah——" he faltered.

Buzzard smiled tolerantly. "It's hard to believe, if you haven't the imagination," he remarked.

Rabbit picked up a stone and tossed it away in a show of distaste. He thought he had plenty of imagination, and it had nothing to do with believing a couple of outlandish tales. He was silent and so Buzzard went on talking in his staid, wise way.

"This'll be a help to your imagination. Years from now, on a day just like this, another rabbit and buzzard may be sitting right here on the mountain talking as we are talking. And the rabbit tells the buzzard about how you scattered a big giant to the winds. Do you think that buzzard will believe the story, unless he's got imagination? He'll laugh and declare no little rabbit could have done anything of the kind."

"But I did do it," protested Rabbit with heat. "You know I did."

Buzzard shrugged his wings conclusively. "The buzzard won't know it for a fact, though, unless he's willing to take the rabbit's word."

A wrinkle creased in Rabbit's forehead. He did not like the notion of a buzzard laughing and doubting what he had done so cleverly. Glowering indignantly Rabbit gazed at the distant landscape. It was just possible, he conceded, that an enormous bird might have flapped his wings and made it. Somebody made it, Rabbit reasoned, and as far as he was concerned the Great Buzzard could take the credit.

"You've convinced me, Buzzard," Rabbit said. "I guess those crawfish gave me a bad start this morning. That's why I had trouble believing the story of the Great Buzzard. It's true, all right. Why, I can close my eyes right now and see him flying over Atagahi and his wings flattening the valley. I'm grateful to him for giving me a dry place for my feet."

"I guess we're all grateful to the Great Buzzard," Buzzard said.

Rabbit laughed nervously and with strained merriment said, "Hah! Hah! I suppose you've got too much imagination ever to have doubted my story about Flint. Hah! Hah!"

Buzzard smiled and said, "Never doubted it once, Rabbit. It's a good story and I like it."

Rabbit deliberated and a forepaw skipped fitfully among some gravel. "What of the other buzzards?" he asked. "Have they as much imagination as you have? Do you think they'll laugh at my story and disbelieve it?"

"I shouldn't think so," said Buzzard. "They'll enjoy it the way I do. I intend telling it to my children when they get older and they'll probably entertain their children with it some day. No, I should say all buzzards will listen eagerly to the tale and be grateful to you, Rabbit."

Rabbit was reassured and took a deep breath of mountain air. Buzzard spread his wings and raised himself to a tree branch.

"The time is flying and so must I," he said. "Ah, a tree is a marvelous place to perch. I'm grateful to the crawfish for providing the land out of which trees grow. Imagine not having a tree to perch in!" Buzzard looked at Rabbit and gave a small cackling laugh, saying, "I forgot you don't perch in trees."

Rabbit smiled half-heartedly. There were those disagreeable little red crawfish back in the conversation again. Well, he didn't have to be grateful to them for anything and he'd never swallow their preposterous story. "No, I don't need trees," he said. "I like them, but I could really get along without them."

Buzzard looked down at Rabbit and put his head reflectively on one side. "Rabbit, I wonder if the trees don't mean more to you than you think they do?" he mused. Then Buzzard flapped his wide wings and lifted himself into the sky. "Good-by," he sang and sailed toward the top of Blood Mountain.

Rabbit watched his departure uneasily. He wished he had not gone so abruptly. That last remark of his made Rabbit feel that Buzzard knew a great deal more than he knew. Did trees mean more to him than he thought they did? Rabbit meditated. He couldn't decide because it was lunch time and he was hungry, and so Rabbit began nibbling grass. With his fourth mouthful he accidentally got a lump of dirt.

"Ugh!" Rabbit exclaimed, spitting it out quickly and putting a forepaw into his mouth to clean off the gritty specks clinging to his teeth. He studied the black bits his paw brought out. "Ugh!" he repeated. "Now, I can believe red crawfish brought up this nasty-tasting stuff. The silly little things! Why didn't they find better dirt while they were about it?"

When Rabbit finished lunching, he sat in the shadow of the trunk of a tree. He missed the cool, refreshing shade of leaves, but that would come in another month. Later on there would be acorns on the oak trees. Yum-yum! Rabbit could almost taste them. He meant to store a lot this year for over next winter. His back began to itch. Rabbit rubbed against the tree trunk. Ummmmm! That felt good and developed some other itchy spots. Ooooo! How nice to have a good back-scratching!

Suddenly Rabbit leaped away from the tree and stared up at it. "A tree!" he exclaimed. "I do need a tree. Gosh! I almost forgot."

And now that he was remembering, it occurred to

him that one winter he had had his warmest home in a trunk hollow. Another time he tunneled a burrow among the roots of a tree where he had a convenient and choice selection of tender young shoots. It was too convenient and Rabbit found himself overeating and he moved away. But he went back often for a nibble.

The little animal patted the tree affectionately.

"I do love you," he said.

Soon afterward Rabbit started down the mountain. He walked slowly because he was thinking of trees, of the earth they grew from, of crawfish, of a big crawfish telling his children about a wicked rabbit who did *not* scatter Flint to the winds, and of a big buzzard with his children grouped about him hearing the true story of Rabbit.

"Oh, well," Rabbit concluded, "somebody had to bring up the land. It could have been crawfish as well as anyone. Better, I suppose, seeing how they pile up mud. Buzzard's a wise bird. He knew I loved trees and if he can believe the story of the crawfish, I might as well. It won't do any harm believing."

But those crawfish children? What could Rabbit do about them? They really should be told the truth.

Late in the afternoon Rabbit approached the spot where he had parted from Terrapin. He came quietly

The Crawfish and the Great Buzzard 123

because he had about figured out a way of making peace with the crawfish and his scheme could not work with noise. Then Rabbit stumbled.

"Ouch!" he squeaked softly.

"Ouch!" the bump squeaked drowsily.

It was Terrapin sleeping beside the pond.

"Shhhh!" whispered Rabbit.

"Oh, hello, Rabbit," said Terrapin hardly awake.

"Goodness me, Terrapin, I thought you'd be home by now. Did I hurt you?"

"Nope, I don't think so," and Terrapin's eyes began to close and his head was sliding into his shell.

"Aren't you going home, Terrapin?"

"I can't. I'm too tired. I've been swimming all day."

"Did you touch bottom?" Rabbit asked.

Terrapin's head shot forward enthusiastically and he opened his eyes wide. "Did I?" he exclaimed brightly. "About a hundred times at least. It was wonderful, but I'm stiff from my first big swim. I couldn't crawl home. I can't even look for my supper, I'm so stiff. Oooooo! I'm hungry and sleepy." The eyes were closing and the head slipping.

"I'll bring you some supper," Rabbit said. "By the way, what do crawfish like to eat?"

"Everything."

Rabbit went looking among the bushes to find things Terrapin would relish. It was nice to have Terrapin sleepy and contented again. Too bad he was stiff, thought Rabbit, but on the other hand it perhaps had helped to get rid of his crankiness. Well, now that Terrapin was feeling better they could have some good times together. He was an excellent friend and he believed Rabbit's story, all right, and Rabbit could count on him to tell his children how true it was.

When Rabbit returned with Terrapin's dinner, the little head was tightly shut away in the shell. Rabbit put down the supper close to the spot where the head would emerge when Terrapin woke.

"He can have his dinner for breakfast," he said.

This occurred on the shore of the pond almost opposite where the crawfish lived. Rabbit walked a way down the shore and then quietly leaped the water. Cautiously he crept back to where the houses were. Not a sound came from within any of them and by the light of the newly risen moon he was pleased to observe no crawfish sentry on duty. This was fine and so Rabbit disappeared among the reeds where he picked up everything he thought would appeal to the appetite of a crawfish. Before each mud tower he stacked a bountiful meal as big as a crawfish house. Then in the mud of the pond's shore he drew a picture of himself, sitting on his hind legs and his forearms flung wide in a friendly gesture. In each forepaw he laid a mound of food.

Then Rabbit scampered swiftly away. His legs felt light and free. He was very happy.

The picture he had made of himself was the same as a letter. Of course, Rabbit didn't know how to write but the crawfish would read his picture as a message something like this:

"Dear Crawfish:
"I bring you gifts. We're friends. I believe the story about your ancestors making the dry land.
"Sincerely yours,
"Rabbit."

Chapter VIII

Rabbit Tricks the Tie Snakes

When two days passed and Terrapin did not come back from the foot of the mountain, Rabbit began to worry. He said that Terrapin could not possibly be swimming and diving all that time, even if he liked it. Either he was lost or he had had an accident. Rabbit let the third day go by, in case Terrapin were crawling unusually slowly, but on the fourth day he started out to look for his missing friend.

Rabbit did not set out eagerly. Searching for Terrapin meant returning to the neighborhood of the crawfish. Perhaps his picture-letter had pleased them and perhaps not. About this Rabbit was content to remain forever in the dark because, despite his generous impulse to make friends with them, the memory of those creeping little red fish sent a shiver along his spine. He thought he would not be disappointed if he never saw a crawfish again.

But with Terrapin lost he had to forget his dislikes and fears. However, it occurred to Rabbit that if he were careful he might manage to sneak up on the crawfish village, have a quiet look, and get away without any of the inhabitants knowing he'd been there. And so Rabbit sneaked and, as he peered from behind the reeds, he saw the crawfish all along the muddy shore of the pond. Some were making their towers higher, some were creaking about in that unsteady gait of theirs, and down close to the water was a group taking their morning exercises. Keeping time with the leader they opened and closed their sharp claws to strengthen the muscles so they could pinch harder.

Rabbit didn't see Terrapin and so he ran from this unattractive scene as fast as he could. Out of earshot of the crawfish, he stopped at the water's edge, leaned over the pond and loudly called Terrapin's name. If he were on the bottom, he might hear and come up. A broadening circle of ripples wrinkled the surface. Something *was* moving underneath, and Rabbit watched expectantly for Terrapin's head to bob up. But it wasn't Terrapin. Tie Snake slid from the pond onto the shore.

"Hello, Rabbit," he said. "Why are you shouting?"

"I'm looking for Terrapin," said Rabbit. "Have you seen him on the bottom?"

"No, but then I only woke up yesterday. Spring came awfully early this year." Tie Snake languidly stretched his long black body and yawned. "Ho-o-o-hummm! The winter was too short. I've never known one to pass so quickly. I could have slept a couple of weeks longer."

"You snakes are lazy," Rabbit teased. "Imagine sleeping all winter and then wanting to sleep some more!"

Tie Snake coiled indignantly. "I'm not lazy," he said. "I wouldn't mind a fight right now. It would really wake me up. I feel strong enough to lick anybody!"

As a fighter Tie Snake had quite a reputation. Animals were very careful not to stir up his wrath. He was a relentless foe, never giving up pursuit until he had tracked down an opponent and punished him. As for other snakes, they either kept on the friendly side of Tie Snake or they kept out of his path.

Now Rabbit should have been warned by the way Tie Snake wound and unwound his body that he was in no mood to be trifled with and he had best leave him alone. But Rabbit was enjoying talking and ruffling up the serpent's temper, slightly he thought, and couldn't resist tantalizing a little more.

"You fight now!" he taunted. "Why you've been asleep all winter. You couldn't be strong enough to last out a good fight."

"Sssssss!" hissed the snake and wriggled toward Rabbit. "I'll show you whether I'm strong!"

Rabbit leaped away. "Now, now, Tie Snake," he said soothingly, "I was only teasing. Of course, you're strong."

"Ssssssss!" repeated the snake. "I'll show you!"

Rabbit scuttled ahead, pleading, "Calm yourself, Tie Snake. I don't want to fight. I haven't time to fight today."

"Sssssss!" said Tie Snake threateningly.

With jerky leaps Rabbit widened the space between him and his short-tempered pursuer. "Please, please," he begged. "Stop a moment. I've got to find Terrapin. He's been lost three days."

Tie Snake stopped. Often he went swimming with Terrapin and they were good friends. Terrapin admired Tie Snake, particularly the way he twisted and untwisted his limber body, an experience forever denied to a rigid shell.

"Terrapin lost!" the snake gasped. "For three days! Gracious, why didn't you say so? Where's he lost?"

Rabbit thought these questions positively idiotic, but merely told of Terrapin's strange disappearance. Tie Snake listened with interest, his unblinking beady eyes staring intently at Rabbit.

"Are you telling the truth?" he demanded suspiciously. "I'm not sure you are. I've heard about your tricks and how clever you think you are. I'll have to take your word you're not lying. Can I have your word?"

"Oh, yes," Rabbit quickly agreed—anything to end this interview.

"Then I won't fight you," Tie Snake announced. "But I'm going to show you how strong I am."

Rabbit began edging away. "All right," he said. "I'll be back tomorrow to see you. I must be off now. Good-by." He took several hurried leaps and heard a familiar rustle at his heels. Rabbit turned and there was Tie Snake, still in pursuit.

"Wait a minute!" the snake commanded. "You can't get away from me so easily. I'm going to show you how strong I am—*right now!*"

Rabbit's heart thumped apprehensively. "Now what?" he asked himself, wishing he had made his last leap longer.

"You go get a thick grapevine," the snake said, "and bring it back here. I'll tie myself onto one end and you can hang onto the other and, we'll pull. I'll drag you all over the place. *Siszszszszh!*" He laughed gloatingly, "I'll show you I'm strong. And how will you like being dragged through the pond? *Szszszszh!* I've heard you don't care for water. *Sszszszh!* Now get that grapevine and no tricks. You come back. Remember I can find your trail no matter where you go. Now get! *Szszszszh!*"

Tie Snake stretched forward as if he would strike Rabbit and Rabbit bounded through the air and was gone. Some minutes later, still running, he rounded a bend in the pond and threw himself panting onto the ground.

"Now, why, of all days, did I have to meet Tie Snake and get into an argument?" he asked. "And poor Terrapin! Lost, and I can't look for him. I've got to look for a grapevine to get myself pulled into the water. Ugh!"

Rabbit looked at the pond with loathing. "Ugh!" he repeated.

The water began to splash furiously.

"Cabbages and lettuce leaves!" Rabbit exclaimed and hopped away. "Now I hope I haven't gone and made the water angry!"

But it was another snake coming ashore. Rabbit thought at first it was Tie Snake on his trail, but this was another tie snake.

"Hello, Rabbit," said the Second Tie Snake. "Nice day. But I'm still sleepy. Never known such a short winter. I only woke up yesterday. Ho-o-o-humm!"

And Rabbit did not tell the Second Tie Snake he was lazy, but said pleasantly, "I hope you had a good rest."

"Not too good," said the Second Tie Snake, "but a beautiful day like this makes me feel like my last year's fighting self. My, I'm strong!"

Rabbit looked at the big black snake rolling his body into loops and thought what a pity this snake and the First Tie Snake couldn't get together for a fight, since both were so eager for one. "Perhaps I could bring them together, if I'm clever," Rabbit thought. "But how?"

"You are strong," he began flatteringly, and Second Tie Snake, encouraged by admiration, made an extra large loop of himself. "My!" exclaimed Rabbit. "I didn't know you could do that. It's wonderful!"

Second Tie Snake lifted his head proudly. "I should like to be stronger," he said. "There's another tie snake up the pond who's as strong as I am. Last year he and I would get a grapevine between us and pull. He couldn't pull me any farther than I could pull him. This year I'd like to be able to drag him along a little way. Wouldn't he be surprised!"

Rabbit stared vacantly at the landscape, preoccupied with his thoughts. All of a sudden his eyes saw what he was staring at. Several yards away the pond curved sharply around a hill. Had Rabbit known his alphabet he would have realized that the pond was shaped like a large letter U. Here was Rabbit sitting on the bank at one side of the U with Second Tie Snake, while just over the ridge out of sight was First Tie Snake waiting for Rabbit to return with a grapevine.

"How'd you like to surprise this other tie snake?" Rabbit asked. "I think if you had a little practice pulling—something to make your muscles firm—you could do it."

"Pulling practice would help," said the snake, "but where can I get it?"

"Practice on me," suggested Rabbit. "I'll get a grapevine and hold it while you pull."

Second Tie Snake sniggered. "Pull against you!" he scoffed. "That wouldn't give me any practice. You'd be nothing to pull against. You haven't any strength."

"I've got more strength than you think," Rabbit boasted. "Of course, I don't pretend to be as strong as you are. Still I could give you practice and it would be good for your muscles. I'd like to help you."

"Practice won't do any harm," agreed Second Tie Snake. "I guess we could try it."

"I'll go find a grapevine," said Rabbit, and he hurried into the woods leaving the serpent coiling and rolling to limber his muscles.

Rabbit wasn't gone long. He came back staggering under the weight of a long, thick, ropey vine that trailed from one narrow shoulder. With a sign of spent endurance he dropped the vine near the water.

"Whewww!" he whistled with exhaustion. "I ought to be stronger for carrying such a load."

Second Tie Snake squeezed his body around the grapevine testing its sturdiness. "It's a good stout vine," he commented. "I don't think it'll break while we're pulling."

Rabbit rested his forepaws on his shanks and pretended to survey the scenery. "Now, let's see," he said, "where'll we put the vine?"

"What's the matter with doing it right here?" the Snake asked.

Rabbit appeared to be lost in thought as he studied the pond and the ridge around which it nearly bent itself double.

"I have a wonderful idea," he said at length. "See that hill there? I'll stretch the vine across it. You stay on this side and pull and I'll go over and pull from the other side. That way I'll be hanging down from the end of the vine and you'll have more weight to pull against. That should make you stronger."

"A good idea," Second Tie Snake agreed. "But to save you the trouble I'll go over the hill and pull from that side. Now let's make haste." And with that Second Tie Snake started up the ridge.

Rabbit darted ahead of him, blocking his way. "No, no, you stay here," he said. "Leave this to me. I've got to measure and divide the vine exactly in half. Now you wait here until I get everything fixed and save your strength for pulling."

The serpent consented and Rabbit climbed the hill

carrying one end of the long vine with him. He measured the length accurately, placed the middle of the vine on the crest of the ridge and extended the two halves down either side. This done he hurried off to find First Tie Snake.

He came upon him almost immediately, for the serpent, impatient with waiting and believing that Rabbit had run off, had started out to look for him.

"Where've you been all this time?" First Tie Snake demanded angrily.

Rabbit turned, leaping away as he replied. "I found such a long and stout vine it was slow work bringing it here. You know, I'm not strong, and my strength gave out. I've dropped the vine on the little hill yonder. See it? I came back here to ask whether you'd mind coming to the hill. We can pull against each other there as well as anywhere."

First Tie Snake could see the heavy vine hanging over the hummock. "Good," he said and began to laugh. "Szszszszh! So your strength gave out and you couldn't carry the vine farther. Szszszszh! I'll have you in the water in no time. Szszszszh!"

Rabbit put a frown on his forehead and tried to appear worried. At this First Tie Snake laughed some more. They hurried to the foot of the ridge. First Tie Snake wasted no time and in a moment had himself coiled tightly about the end of the grapevine.

"Go on over on the other side and take hold," he said to Rabbit.

"All right. I'll shout 'Yoo-hoo' when I'm ready to pull." So saying, Rabbit scampered up the hill and down the other side where he found Second Tie Snake securely wound about his end of the vine.

"Everything is ready," announced Rabbit. "I'll go back over the hill and when I shout 'Yoo-hoo' you pull. Don't be surprised if you discover me rather strong."

"I hope you are strong," said Second Tie Snake. "I want to develop my muscles."

Rabbit skipped blithely up the ridge again. As he neared the top he slowed down and went ahead cautiously. On the very top he saw a tuft of grass. He crept into it and peering out between the leaves looked down first one slope of the hill and then the other. "Szszszszh!" he hissed softly to himself, imitating the snakes. From his hiding-place Rabbit could see both serpents, though neither of them could see him. First Tie Snake had shifted coils to get a firmer grip. "That's to drag me into the water sooner." Rabbit smiled. Second Tie Snake had taken another loop about his end of the grapevine. "And you'll need it, too," thought Rabbit.

Rabbit crouched low in the grass and put his paws to his mouth to give the signal.

"Yoo-hooooo!"

With a good healthy grunt First Tie Snake gave the vine a mighty yank. Second Tie Snake was not prepared for any such display of strength at the other end of the vine and would have been jerked half-way up the hill had not he, also, given a powerful yank to the vine at the very same moment. The same thought was in the heads of both snakes: to pull Rabbit over the hill and into the water as quickly as possible and teach him a lesson for being so bold as to try to match his feeble strength with that of a muscular tie snake.

Both were mightily surprised. First Tie Snake hissed with anger and hurt pride and settled down to pull with all his might. Second Tie Snake did exactly the same. As their strength was evenly matched the vine tightened and creaked from the strain on it, but hardly moved at all.

Rabbit would have loved to watch the contest a while longer but was afraid to. His insides were burning up with the laughter he dared not let out. So, slipping through the grass quietly, he left the toiling, grunting snakes who were getting angrier every moment and filling the air with their hisses.

When a safe distance away, Rabbit began to run as fast as his fleet legs would carry him. He headed for the forest and did not stop until deep within its protecting shadows. Then he laughed and laughed and laughed.

"I'd like to see those two snakes when they find out the trick I played on them," he said. "Ha! Ha! Won't they want to get hold of me? But they never will for I'll never go near the pond again as long as I live. Ha! Ha! That was a narrow escape, but I guess I was pretty clever. Wait'll I see Terrapin and tell him about it."

Rabbit's mirth ended suddenly. "Terrapin!" he exclaimed. "I'd forgotten! He's lost! I must find him!"

Frantically Rabbit rushed through the woods, looking behind trees, spinning around rocks, scraping his coat in underbrush and pausing often to call, "Terrapin! Terrapin!"

After hours of weary search and calling Rabbit heard a queer little singsong voice. He listened, but decided the voice was not raised in answer to his calls. No one who was lost would reply with such a squeaky, silly song as he heard coming through the woods. Maybe it was a bird, Rabbit thought. Funny, he'd never heard a bird with a voice like it. The voice was singing too high and the song was tuneless. Rabbit came closer and made out the words of the song.

I will give you my blood
I will give you my fat
Anything you wish
Please help me mend my back.

An absurd song! Even the rhyme was bad.

"The bird must be hurt," Rabbit thought. "Poor thing! I'll help him." And he ran toward the voice. He stopped in amazement. The voice didn't belong to a bird. Before him squatted Terrapin with his shell smashed to bits.

"Terrapin! Terrapin!" said Rabbit, dropping close beside his friend. "Whatever has happened to you?"

"Oh, Rabbit, look at my back!" Terrapin sobbed. "It's broken. I can't move."

Rabbit ran a paw tenderly over the shell. It was a hodgepodge of chips and cracks, and Terrapin's eyes were very red and swollen, as if he had been crying for a long time. "Poor little Terrapin," Rabbit said once more, and tears of sympathy came into his eyes.

"A big rock fell on me," said Terrapin. "I shouldn't ever come into the woods. I belong near the water. Now my life is ruined. I'll never be able to crawl again." And fresh tears gushed from his red eyes.

"There, there, Terrapin, maybe I can fix you up," Rabbit comforted him.

Terrapin's crying dwindled to sniffles and he asked hopefully, "How?"

Rabbit scratched behind an ear and he examined the toes of his hind legs. He was thinking hard but as yet he had no idea as to how to fix Terrapin's back. Meantime, he'd tell him a story to take his mind off his hurt. Terrapin was always wanting to hear stories. He'd tell him how clever he had been with the tie snakes.

"Terrapin, you should have been with me this morning," he began with a burst of enthusiasm. "I've certainly shown Tie Snake he can't get the best of me. You'll have a good laugh over this story. I was coming along this morning and——"

"Can you fix my back?" Terrapin interrupted.

"I guess so," said Rabbit. "But, Terrapin, this was so funny. I was coming along——"

"Fix my back, please," Terrapin whined. This was one time he didn't care to hear a story.

Rabbit walked thoughtfully around the broken shell, tapping it and looking into the many cracks.

"I might be able to stick your shell together with some of that gum that drips from the pine tree," he said. "It should work. Anyway I can try. You never know what you can do until you try. Tie Snake had me stumped for a moment this morning, but I———"

"There's a pine tree behind you," said Terrapin.

Rabbit hopped over to the tree and began plucking off the drops of gum that oozed through the bark. "Poor Terrapin," he said. "I hope I can patch him up. It'll take a long time, but I'll tell him about the tie snakes while I'm working and that'll make the time go faster."

With two wads of the gum Rabbit returned to Terrapin and prepared to mend the broken shell.

"Hold still now," he advised.

Terrapin held ever so still, hardly daring to take a breath. Rabbit brought two pieces of shell back into place and rubbed the gum between them. It held them fast together. Then he giggled. "If I'd only thought to rub pine gum on that grapevine," he said. "Ha! Ha! Imagine it, Terrapin! Those two snakes wound all around it and *stuck!*"

"Hurry, I'm so uncomfortable," said Terrapin.

Rabbit was still chuckling and his paw wavered as he shifted a piece of shell and applied the gum.

"Ouch!" screamed Terrapin. "Take it out! Take it out! That's the wrong place!"

Soberly Rabbit put the fragment of shell in its proper place and then stood off a little way to look at what he had done so far.

"It's not bad, Terrapin," he said. "You'll have a nice back when I get through." Rabbit cocked his head critically. "You know, I think I'm going to like it better than your old back. You'll have rows of checks—squares almost. Makes a nice design. Your other back was too plain. Of course, the way your shell's broken I can't make the cracks run in exactly straight lines, but——"

"Cracks!" Terrapin exclaimed in alarm. "Are there going to be cracks in me? How'll I swim? The water'll come in and I'll sink!"

"Oh, no, Terrapin. These are closed cracks. No water'll get inside."

Terrapin writhed impatiently and sniffled. "Well, stop standing around," he said irritably. "Get busy and finish. I want to crawl once more."

Rabbit stepped closer to his work. It was tedious, and went slowly. Poor little Terrapin! He was tired and feeling wretched. Again Rabbit decided to entertain him.

" 'Szszszszsh!' " he mimicked. "That's the way those snakes laughed. Imagine laughing that way, Terrapin. I bet they're not laughing now. You should have——"

"Please, Rabbit, keep your mind on what you're doing," said Terrapin. "You'll get another piece in wrong. Besides, I don't think this is the time to talk about laughing."

It was no use. Rabbit gave up and finished patching the shell in silence.

"There you are, Terrapin," he said at last. "See if you can crawl."

Terrapin could crawl.

"Oooooo, Rabbit!" he exclaimed happily. "Watch me! Oooooo! It feels good to move. I'd never know my back was broken. It doesn't even creak when I crawl. Ooooo! I'm moving."

Rabbit was looking at his patchwork admiringly. He thought he had done well. "You've got a beautiful back now," he said. "Too bad you can't see it."

"Ooooo, I don't care," said Terrapin. "I just want to crawl and crawl. Come on, Rabbit. Let's go."

Terrapin was headed toward the pond.

"Not that way, Terrapin," said Rabbit. "Let's go home through the woods."

"But I want to go down to the water for a swim," said Terrapin. "Besides I've got to wash my eyes. They feel awfully red from crying. Come with me to the pond."

"Oh, no, I can't," said Rabbit, jumping a few steps in the other direction.

"Why not?" Terrapin asked.

"I don't want to," said Rabbit truthfully.

And so they parted, Rabbit hurrying toward his burrow far from the water, and Terrapin, immensely happy to be crawling again, bound for a swim and to wash the red from his eyes. He promised to be careful of falling rocks and to come to supper presently with Rabbit.

Terrapin approached the pond from the ridge over which Rabbit had hung the grapevine. As he came near he heard the vine creaking. Looking down both sides of the hill he saw the two snakes straining against each other.

"Szszszszh!" hissed First Tie Snake and tugged with all his might.

"Szszszszsh!" hissed Second Tie Snake and yielded not an inch.

"Ggrr—runk!" groaned the grapevine wearily.

Terrapin watched the battle in bewilderment.

"What kind of game is this?" he asked himself.

"*Grr—unk—ss—rah!*" groaned the vine and snapped in two.

With a great splash the snakes fell back into the water which must have cooled their tempers or else scared them, for from the hill Terrapin saw them gliding through the pond, swimming away from each other as fast as they could go.

"What are those snakes up to?" Terrapin was still puzzled. "It must be a new game. I'll have to remember to ask Rabbit about it. He ought to know what game they were playing."

According to the Indians' story, Terrapin dove and swam for a long, long while, but he never washed the red from his eyes and terrapins' eyes nowadays always look as if they were red from weeping. The new back of checks that Rabbit gave Terrapin must have been an improvement for terrapins since then have worn no other.

Chapter IX

Turkey's Singing Lesson

Tie Snake was a bully and so the animals laughed heartily over the neat trick that Rabbit had played on him. Thus it was that once again Rabbit found himself a hero in Atagahi. He enjoyed it and fell to talking a great deal, boasting and swaggering about until Black Bear, the leader of the animals, scratched his chin in thought and wondered what he should do to make Rabbit a little more modest and proper in his behavior.

But Black Bear didn't have to do anything because Wildcat came along and showed Rabbit a thing or two which made him less talkative. The funny part of this was that Rabbit brought it all on himself. He began by trying to trick Wildcat. This is the way it happened.

Hopping leisurely down a trail early one morning, feeling very well pleased with himself, Rabbit came upon some fresh footprints in the soft earth. Although he stooped down and examined them closely Rabbit could not, for the life of him, figure out whose tracks they were. There was one thing about the footprints that interested him especially.

"The animal who made these," observed Rabbit, "hasn't any claws, only pads. If I can find him I ought to have some fun. For I've got claws."

Rabbit hastened along the trail, following the strange footprints and eventually overtook Wildcat whom he knew only slightly because Wildcat prowled at night while Rabbit slept.

The two animals greeted each other and then Rabbit suggested that they play a game.

"All right," agreed Wildcat. "I love to play. Shall we chase a leaf?"

"Oh, no," said Rabbit. "I know a new game called Slap. I'll teach it to you. First I slap you with my paw like this"—Rabbit gently tapped Wildcat, careful not to let him feel the tips of his claws—"and then you slap me. The idea is to see who gets slapped down. And, of course, you must try to duck away from my slaps and not get hit."

Wildcat lazily blinked his eyes to hide the look of suspicion that began to come into them. The woods were full of tales of Rabbit's cleverness, and Wildcat had heard of the joke on Tie Snake. He wondered what sort of trick Rabbit might be up to now, proposing *this* sort of game, for no animal in the forest slapped and dodged so expertly as Wildcat.

But Rabbit, for all his busybody ways of learning things about his companions in Atagahi, did not know this. Rabbit's idea was to surprise Wildcat by scratching him just a little at first, and when Wildcat flinched to express amazement that such a little tap should hurt, and promise not to slap so hard any more. This, Rabbit thought, would surely make a big animal like Wildcat feel ashamed and reckon Rabbit a mighty powerful fellow for his size.

"It sounds like an entertaining game," said Wildcat languidly.

"I'll count one, two, three and say, '*Go!*' and then we begin slapping," instructed Rabbit.

He counted and said, "*Go!*" at the same time pretending to slap with his right paw, but really striking out with his left. This simple trick Wildcat had learned from his mother when he was a tiny kitten with eyes barely open. Gracefully he moved his head out of the way of Rabbit's blow. Then he pretended to slap with his right and *did* slap with it, knocking Rabbit flat. As Rabbit fell sprawling something sharper than the thorns of a blackberry bush pricked his side.

"Ow-w-w-w!" howled Rabbit, catching his side.

Wildcat had heard such screams before. They didn't interest him. He lay down on the ground and began licking his paws. Stray bits of fur from Rabbit's coat were wedged between the pads. Wildcat stretched his paws and began to lick this fur away. As he stretched, long, shining, needle-like claws protruded from beneath each pad. Rabbit was so astonished he forgot about the pain in his side.

"Cabbages and lettuce leaves! Where did you get those claws?"

Wildcat half closed his eyes and said drowsily, "I've had them longer than I can remember."

"Where do you keep them? They don't show in your footprints."

"Of course not," said Wildcat. "I take good care of my claws. If I walked on them, the points would be blunted. When walking I tuck my claws up inside my skin."

Rabbit wagged his head slowly. "You certainly fooled me," he admitted. "I didn't think you had claws. Oooh! that's an ugly scratch you gave me. It hurts."

The corners of Wildcat's mouth lifted mockingly. "You expected to fool me," he said. "If you were really smart, you'd know I'm much too sly an animal to be fooled by a rabbit."

"But I *am* really smart," asserted Rabbit.

A self-satisfied grin widened Wildcat's mouth. "Mmmmmm!" he sniffed. "I'm unconvinced."

"Then I'll convince you," said Rabbit emphatically.

Wildcat said nothing. He grinned again, though, which said as plain as anything what he was thinking.

"I'll show you that I'm smart," said Rabbit furiously, and he ran off so he couldn't see Wildcat's grinning.

He spent the remainder of the day wandering aimlessly along the paths and thinking hard how to "show" Wildcat. He tried to avoid the other animals. Late in the afternoon when he met Black Bear all Rabbit said was, "Hello," and marched right on with his gloomy thoughts. Black Bear stared after him, a little puzzled, but immensely pleased that Rabbit hadn't stopped to tell some boastful story. "Perhaps," said Black Bear to himself, "I shan't have to punish him after all."

Meanwhile Terrapin, having recovered from his broken back, met with another unfortunate adventure. Strolling through the woods, he had come upon an attractive red bag. Delighted with his find, he hung it around his neck and hastened home to put it away for the next ball play. At last he had something to dress up in. To be sure the bag was much too large for him, but Terrapin knew Rabbit would help him make it the right size. When he was almost home he met Turkey who burst into laughter at the sight of the big bag trailing from Terrapin's small neck, and tripping him at every step.

"Well, Terrapin, what are you doing now?" Turkey asked.

"I found a red bag. Isn't it beautiful?" said Terrapin enthusiastically.

"It is pretty, but too large for you," said Turkey.

"It'll be all right after Rabbit makes it smaller," said Terrapin.

"Let me try it on," Turkey suggested.

Terrapin handed over his bag agreeably. "It should fit you," he said.

Turkey hung the red bag over his neck and thought the color looked exceedingly well against a background of dark feathers. He opened his fan-shaped tail, puffed out his chest and strutted.

Terrapin thought the bird looked real handsome and his eyes gleamed with generous admiration. "My, but you do look grand with that bag," he said. "It gives me an idea of the way I'll look when I wear it."

Turkey was liking the bag so much that he thought he wanted to keep it. He might talk Terrapin into giving it to him, but decided he'd just run off with it. Terrapin couldn't catch him. And so he walked ahead a little way, turned and pulled the bag around so that it hung directly beneath his beak. He asked, "Terrapin, how do you like the bag worn this way?"

Terrapin studied the new effect. "I think I like it best that way, Turkey," he replied. "It's actually more becoming."

"Thanks," said Turkey. "That's the way I'll always wear it." And Turkey started running off.

Terrapin looked dazed. "Come back," he shouted. "Give me my bag!"

"It's mine now," Turkey called back.

Terrapin tried to run after him, but it was no use. His short legs could never catch up with the great bird. He turned around and kicked some stones at him, which was Terrapin's way of fighting. A few of the stones struck Turkey's legs.

"Ouch!" he screeched and began to limp. Even so, his limp was still too fast for Terrapin's crawl and he made off with the bright-colored bag.

Saddened by his loss Terrapin went to look for Rabbit. Rabbit was sitting under a tree still brooding over Wildcat's mocking grin. He listened to Terrapin's story about the stolen bag and said, "Well, we'll have to teach Mr. Turkey a lesson."

"Teach Turkey a lesson!" a voice shrilled from the tree and with that peculiar roaring, drum-drumming of his wings, Grouse swooped to the ground, bouncing with resentment. "I'm Turkey's teacher. I give him singing lessons and he gives me feathers for the ruff I'm making around my neck. I'll thank you not to try teaching him anything. I haven't enough feathers yet!"

For the first time Rabbit and Terrapin noticed the new feather collar Grouse was wearing. It looked rather nice on him, though skimpy. It was true; he needed more plumage to fill it out.

"We don't want to give Turkey singing lessons. We can't sing," said Rabbit.

"What do you want?" asked Grouse.

"Terrapin, tell Grouse about your red bag," said Rabbit.

When Grouse heard the story, he was indignant over Turkey's theft. "What a wicked bird!" he said. "And poor little Terrapin! To steal from you! It's a shame. Turkey ought to be punished. I'm not sure that I care to have any more of his feathers around my neck."

"Oh, I would," Rabbit advised. "Your ruff needs thickening, and I for one wouldn't like mixing in a different sort of feather. You'll have to take more of Turkey's."

Grouse thought it over. "Well, perhaps you're right," he said in his quick, positive manner. "But I know what I'll do. I'll get the feathers I need and then I'll ruin Turkey's voice. The vain old bird wants to sing more than anything else. I'll give him a lesson. I'll teach him not to steal."

"That's great," said Rabbit eagerly.

"Oooooo," gurgled Terrapin happily.

"How'll you do it?" asked Rabbit.

Grouse already had a clear plan. "Turkey'll be along soon for his lesson," he said. "You hide in the bushes over there and watch me. Don't make any noise. Now get over there and hide. Shooo!"

With a whir-r-r-ring of his strong wings, Grouse hustled Rabbit and Terrapin into the hiding-place. Rabbit wished he wouldn't make that noise with his wings. He had never cared for the sound. There was something so startling about it. Terrapin had the same feeling and he tried to crawl so fast he stumbled and nearly rolled over on his back. He scrambled into the bushes all out of breath and gasping noisily.

"Ssshhh!" warned Grouse.

Turkey came limping along with his chest proudly expanded. Beneath his chin swayed the red bag.

"Goodness me, you're all dressed up today," Grouse greeted him. "What a lovely collar! Oh, dear, I wish my collar were finished. If my throat had been wrapped up good last night I shouldn't be hoarse to-day."

"Well, give me my lesson and I'll give you more feathers," said Turkey.

"No lesson today, Turkey. I can't sing. I've got a sore throat." And Grouse coughed a huge cough.

"Please, Grouse. With my new red collar I feel happy enough to sing."

"I haven't a collar, but I have a bad throat and I don't feel happy enough to sing."

Turkey snatched out a clawful of quills and offered them to Grouse. "Here, I'll give you the rest of the feathers now if you'll give me a lesson today."

The bird's eyes shone with pleasure as he accepted the feathers and poked them into the gaps in his ruff. In the bushes Rabbit and Terrapin agreed that the collar made Grouse a handsome bird.

Grouse pretended to clear his throat and then sounded a few notes.

"Ahem!" he coughed again. "My throat feels better already. Perhaps I can give you a lesson after all. Stand on that rock over there. I'll stand on this hollow log. I'll give you a note and when I beat on the log with my tail you try to sing the same note as loud as you can."

Turkey mounted the rock and from the log came a high shrill note. Then came the dum-dum beat of Grouse's tail against the log. Turkey sang back loudly.

"No, no, that isn't the note I gave you," Grouse complained. "Pitch your voice higher. Like this."

A shrill note again sounded in a higher key. Then Grouse signaled with his tail.

Turkey's voice struggled upward but cracked with the effort. Then Grouse sounded even higher notes.

The vain Turkey tried to reproduce them, straining and straining his voice until the only noise he could make was a broken "Gobble, gobble, gobble."

This unmusical noise sounded very funny to Rabbit and Terrapin who started giggling in their hiding-place.

"There now, I've ruined your voice," Grouse announced. "That's to punish you for taking Terrapin's red bag."

Terrapin and Rabbit came out of the bushes laughing.

"Gobble, gobble, gobble," mimicked Rabbit.

"Gobble, gobble, gobble," said Terrapin, and they laughed some more.

Turkey stood on the rock, a sorry-looking sight. His fan-tail folded and drooped and his chest was no longer swollen with pride. He seemed ready to cry.

"I'll give Terrapin back his bag, if you'll give me back my voice." He spoke hoarsely to Grouse.

"Too late now," said Grouse. "You'll never sing. Your singing voice is gone forever."

Wailing, "Gobble, gobble, gobble," Turkey fluttered from the rock and limped off into the woods.

Terrapin and Rabbit thanked Grouse for Turkey's lesson.

"We enjoyed it," said Terrapin and laughed. "Gobble, gobble, gobble. Did you ever hear anything funnier?"

Both Rabbit and Grouse agreed that they had never heard anything funnier in their lives.

"I do like your new ruff, Grouse," said Rabbit after a while. "I hope you'll wear it always."

"I think I will," said Grouse. "It really is a protection for my throat." With that startling burr-r-r-r of his wings, Grouse flew off shrilling, "Good-by."

Terrapin and Rabbit waved after him until he was out of sight which was not long, for Grouse flew swiftly. Terrapin giggled and said, "Gobble, gobble, gobble," but Rabbit did not laugh any more. He sighed, and sat down underneath the tree and resumed his brooding. He still had to show Wildcat.

And so now you know how the Indians believe that turkeys acquired their red wattles and grouses their fluffy neckruffs.

Chapter X

Rabbit Shows Wildcat

SEVERAL times a day Terrapin asked Rabbit about the scratches on his side, how he got them and why and when, but Rabbit never told him the true story.

"I had an accident in the woods," he'd answer.

"How?" asked Terrapin.

Rabbit hesitated. "Er—a—a twig caught my coat and tore it," he replied.

"Oooooo!" cooed Terrapin. "What a strong twig! I don't want it to scratch my back. Will you show me where the twig is?"

"Uh-huh," agreed Rabbit absently, with his mind on other matters.

Terrapin began to crawl. "Come on," he urged. "Let's go look at the twig."

Rabbit frowned and stammered, "Uh—er—uh—not right now. Another time. I'm thinking."

"Tch! You're always thinking."

Of late, this was certainly a fact. Thinking up a way to show Wildcat that he was smart wasn't simple because Rabbit had to find a good safe trick. He wanted no more painful scratches. After a week his wounds were just beginning to heal. The skin had grown together leaving three lumpy red lines, but not a single strand of fur sprouted on them. Hopefully Rabbit examined them morning, noon and night, and he began to fear the scars would forever remain bald. They were not a pretty sight.

The Horned Green Beetle helped Rabbit in a small way to settle finally on a plan for dealing with Wildcat. Rabbit was walking down the River Path one morning when he heard a clinking, brassy sound like *"Branlk-wham!"* He recognized it at once. Beetle never looks where he's flying and he's always banging into everything. He has a spot on his forehead which he has bumped so often that the color is rubbed off. Apparently his bumps do not hurt him and so Rabbit did not say sympathetically, "Poor Horned Green Beetle!"

He looked instead with great interest at the tree with which Beetle collided. It was a bent, stooped tree that leaned across the River Path as if it might topple over any moment.

"That's the tree I want," said Rabbit, "and it's on

the River Path, just where I need it. Nearly all Atagahi passes this way."

The next morning Rabbit slipped away before breakfast to show Wildcat. He started early so as not to awaken Terrapin who was in excellent health these days and most surely would have asked questions and wanted to go with him. Rabbit had not got far on his way when he met pouchy-cheeked Chipmunk rushing about industriously to collect himself more breakfast than he could eat. He always stored what was left over and this kept him plump during winter.

"Good morning, Chipmunk."

"Good morning, Rabbit."

A pleasant odor brushed the tip of Rabbit's nose. "Ummmm!" he sniffed. "What's that? Smells like you've a delicious breakfast."

"Water-lily roots," said Chipmunk. "I found my first of the season this morning."

"Ummmm!" repeated Rabbit, breathing deep of the lily-root scented air. He, too, loved water-lily roots, and rarely had them. They grew in the water, of course, and unless he found them around the edge of a pond, they were out of Rabbit's reach. Chipmunk didn't like water either and so Rabbit knew he had taken all the roots near the bank. Chipmunk was like that. He carried off all the food he found, putting away what he couldn't eat in those countless tunnels he dug underground. Under the circumstances, Rabbit decided the only way for him to get water-lily roots for breakfast was to flatter and wheedle Chipmunk.

"What a pretty coat you have, Chipmunk," he began. "It's new, isn't it?"

"Do you like it really?" Chipmunk asked, and scampered up and down in front of Rabbit showing off his coat.

"Indeed I do," said Rabbit. "But those stripes down your back—I don't remember them. Where did they come from? They're awfully nice."

"Yes, they're new," said Chipmunk. "I can't make up my mind whether I like them."

"They're a good color," Rabbit said. "I like the black lines with the yellow. They go well together. Oh, yes, I prefer the stripes to your plain old brown coat."

Chipmunk sighed resignedly. "Then I guess I'll start liking the stripes, if you approve. But I don't care for the way I got them. Wildcat gave them to me."

Rabbit sat up with a jolt of surprise. "Wildcat!" he exclaimed.

"Yes, Wildcat," Chipmunk affirmed. "An annoying beast. Whenever he sees me running around, he gets playful and chases me. I don't care to play with Wildcat. He's too rough. One day he slipped up on me. I didn't hear him coming on those padded paws of his—you know how they are."

"I certainly do," said Rabbit, nodding emphatically.

"I started running and Wildcat reached out with his paw to catch me. I got away, but his claws scraped over my back. Ooo-ouch! Did they scratch! They left three deep gashes that were a long time healing. When they did, the hair on my back grew back a different color—the yellow and black streaks you see there now."

"Cabbages and lettuce leaves!" exclaimed Rabbit and in alarm examined his three wounds. "Do you suppose I'll grow yellow and black stripes on my side?"

There was no sign of anything growing yet, and now that he had admitted for the first time to anyone that Wildcat had scratched him, Rabbit sat down and told Chipmunk all about it.

"I'm on my way to show Wildcat right now that I can be smart," he concluded. "I've got a good trick planned for him."

"I'm glad to hear that," said Chipmunk. "And I hope your trick is really good. It's time somebody did something to Wildcat. Goodness me! If he scratches like this in play, what would he do if he ever got real angry! Tell me about your trick."

Rabbit was just about to begin when he got another whiff of the water-lily roots. Ummmmm, but they smelled good and Rabbit hadn't had breakfast yet. He sniffed the pungent air, looked slyly at Chipmunk and said, "I haven't time to tell you now. I've got to find myself some breakfast. Too bad, because I'm sure you'd enjoy hearing what I intend to do to Wildcat."

"Goodness me!" said Chipmunk and began to bustle about. "Are you hungry? Why didn't you say so? You just come along to my south tunnel and I'll feed you up. Would you care for a breakfast of water-lily roots? They should be good for you—give you lots of energy to use on Wildcat."

Chipmunk proved a generous host, bringing up from his south tunnel storehouse as much food as Rabbit could consume, and dancing attendance to see that Rabbit ate heartily so he would be in fine shape to meet Wildcat. Rabbit enjoyed the smell of the water-lily roots almost as much as their taste.

"Hummmm, isn't that a lovely scent!" he breathed.

"Yes, it is," agreed Chipmunk, "but I know a better one. I had a piece of cheese once. Ummmm! Now there's a grand smell."

Rabbit shook his head with a little shudder of distaste. "No, too smelly. I don't care for it. I think I prefer to smell green things best of all. No color smells better than green. It has a sweet, clean growing odor."

Breakfast over, Rabbit rewarded his little host by telling him about the trick for Wildcat.

"Very clever," commented Chipmunk.

"Do you think it's safe enough? I don't want to get any more scratches."

Chipmunk considered. "Well, I don't know," he said dubiously. "It sounds safe, but then Wildcat is awfully quick. I'd suggest if you feel he's going to scratch, you keep your unscratched side toward him. Your coat'll look better with scratches to match on both sides."

Rabbit rubbed his scars uneasily. Chipmunk wasn't encouraging. Turn his other side to Wildcat for scratching? Indeed! Rather than get hurt again Rabbit thought it might be better to wait until he had a trick that was entirely safe. Scratched again! No sir, decided Rabbit. As it was he couldn't tell yet what color fur he'd sprout, if any ever did sprout. He didn't think he'd like yellow and black stripes along his side. Rabbit wanted the same color he had before.

His problem now was how to back out of the whole business without offending Chipmunk. After all Chipmunk had given him a delicious meal on which to face Wildcat. Chipmunk was apt to misunderstand and think he had been tricked out of a breakfast of water-lily roots. But Rabbit could think of no way of backing out. Perhaps if he sat around something would turn up and so he was in no haste to depart.

"Gracious, my scratches itch," he said, rubbing his side.

"That's a good sign," said Chipmunk. "They're healing. Mine were just like that. Here, let me rub 'em for you."

Rabbit stretched out on his good side and relaxed comfortably while Chipmunk ran his small paws over the scars. Full of good food Rabbit was ready to fall asleep which was a far more pleasant way to spend the time than going out to meet scratchy Wildcat. So Rabbit dozed, and woke up with Chipmunk shouting:

"Rabbit, Rabbit! Look—look what I've found. Your new hair is growing. Look!" Chipmunk had brushed Rabbit's fur away from his wounds and his eyes danced with excitement as he poked a paw along the lumpy, red scratches.

Rabbit didn't stir. He wasn't excited. He had nothing to look forward to anyway. The new fur was probably yellow and black. Rabbit lay back and asked drearily, "What color is it?"

Chipmunk twisted his head and stooped to catch the best light on the little hairs. He counted them. "One, two, three, four—yes, there are *five*. My, they're hard to see!"

Rabbit wasn't excited, but he asked impatiently, "What color are they?"

"It's hard to tell," said Chipmunk slowly. "I don't know. Maybe—oh, I'm not sure."

Rabbit squirmed over the delay. "What color?"

"Wait a minute," commanded Chipmunk. "That's a better light. Let's see. Oooooh, Rabbit! What do you think? They're the same color as your coat."

Rabbit leaped into the air.

"Whoopee!" he shouted joyfully. "Whoopee!" Then he stopped still, his elation gone. "Are you sure,

Chipmunk, are you sure they're the same color? Look again."

Chipmunk looked closely and said he was positive they were the same color.

"Whoopee!" Rabbit shouted. "Oh, Chipmunk, that's good news! My coat's not ruined. Good-by, and thanks for the breakfast. I'm going down the River Path and find Wildcat. Just let me meet him now! Whoopee! Good-by!"

With a leap Rabbit was gone. Chipmunk waved his paw in farewell, but he didn't think Rabbit saw him because he was in such a hurry to meet Wildcat that he didn't look back once.

Rabbit ran all the way to the bent, stooped tree. He looked at the tracks in the River Path and picked out Wildcat's footprints. They pointed in the direction of the River. Wildcat had passed by already on his way for his morning drink of water. He'd be returning soon and so Rabbit sat under the tree and waited.

When he saw Wildcat coming far down the trail his heart began to pitter-patter very fast and his legs wanted him to skip off. But Rabbit stamped them firmly on the ground and told them he wasn't going to run away, even though he was a little afraid of Wildcat.

As Wildcat approached he saw Rabbit standing on

his sturdy hind legs leaning with all his might against the trunk of the bent, stooped tree.

"Quick, Wildcat, help me," Rabbit called. "This tree is about to fall over and block the River Path."

Now every animal in the woods was careful to keep the way open to the water. Black Bear had issued orders saying it was everyone's duty to prevent any blocking of the River Path. And so Wildcat obligingly said, "All right," and shoved his weight against the tree.

With an exaggerated sign of exhaustion, Rabbit removed his shoulder and surrendered the complete burden to Wildcat. "Whew!" He blew out a big breath. "I couldn't have held out much longer. There doesn't seem to be anyone using this trail this morning. Do you think you're strong enough to hold up the tree alone?"

"Of course I am," said Wildcat a trifle indignantly and pushed harder against the trunk.

"Then you stay here while I look for something to brace it," said Rabbit. "Be careful. Don't let the tree fall over."

Rabbit ran back over the path and when he thought he wouldn't be heard, he laughed. Didn't Wildcat look silly standing there wearing himself out to hold up a tree whose roots were fast and deep in the ground?

His trick had succeeded entirely without a scratch!

"Now, Mr. Wildcat, who's the smarter?" Rabbit asked of the trees around him. "I guess that shows you I'm smart."

A rustling in the underbrush startled Rabbit. "It's Wildcat!" he said in a panic. But it was Chipmunk who had followed Rabbit over the River Path, consumed with curiosity to know how the trick was going. Rabbit said, "Come with me," and the two went noiselessly to a rock from behind which they could peek at Wildcat straining against the tree.

Chipmunk tittered.

"Sshshhh!" cautioned Rabbit and himself chuckled.

"Ssshhhsh!" cautioned Chipmunk. "Don't spoil it all before we get a crowd."

In a few minutes Ground Squirrel scampered down the trail and in a whisper Rabbit called to her. Ground Squirrel heard his story, peered at the wearying Wildcat and giggled.

"Ssshshsh!" said Rabbit, and Chipmunk clapped a paw over her mouth, although he too was giggling.

Presently Red Fox came, then Deer, and then Brown Bear, and the snickers of the peeping party concealed behind the rocks were hard to check. Busy little Wren flew overhead and it wasn't long before she spread the story among her friends and flocks of birds darkened the sky, clucking and jabbering, which was their way of laughing at a good joke.

Wildcat was nearly spent with exertion. At last he had to give up. He slumped exhausted to the ground, expecting the bent tree to slump right after him. But there it stood, as stooped as always, but firmly planted in the earth. Wildcat stared in amazement.

"Grrrrr!" he growled as it began to dawn on him he was the victim of a trick.

His amazement and his growl were too much for

the chuckling party behind the rock. They laughed out loud. Brown Bear simply roared and Wildcat glanced in the direction of the roar. He saw Rabbit, holding his sides and laughing hardest of all. Every animal and bird in Atagahi, it seemed, was there, laughing at his stupidity and undoubtedly thinking how clever Rabbit was.

"Grrrrr-sssst!" Wildcat growled and spat, which the animals apparently thought exceedingly funny. They burst into fresh spasms of laughter. Wildcat got up to chase them off and discovered he was too tired to run.

"Grrrrr!" he spat again and dragged himself into the bushes where he couldn't see or hear himself being laughed at.

Chapter XI

Wolf Upsets Terrapin

Terrapin heard the birds twittering, "Rabbit's playing a good joke on Wildcat along the River Path. Come and see it." And he set out to see. But the bent, stooped tree was a long crawl for him and in the afternoon he met the animals, laughing and roaring, as they returned from the scene of Rabbit's revenge on Wildcat. They were so busy talking that none saw the little shell, dusty, hot and leg-weary. Terrapin called, "Hi there!" to Rabbit, but he couldn't make himself heard. For fear of being trampled, he scrambled off the path and into the grass and let the noisy procession go by. He was so disappointed to have missed all the fun after coming such a distance that he lacked the spirit for crawling any more that day, and eventually without supper, he fell asleep where he was.

Terrapin woke the next morning very hungry and, when he stood up on his four legs, he let out a squeal of pain. Stiff and sore from his hike of the day before, Terrapin squatted again and thought he'd rather miss his breakfast than walk for it.

Terrapin had not stirred from his tracks when presently Gray Squirrel came along.

"Good morning, Terrapin," he said, beaming because it was a lovely morning. "How are you? I feel wonderful today. This is the first time I've seen you this season."

Terrapin squirmed irritably. "That's your fault, not mine," he said crossly. "You're always up a tree."

Gray Squirrel jerked his fluffy tail and sat up on his hind legs with his forepaws crossed restfully over his chest. "Yes, it is my fault," he admitted agreeably. "But now that we've met, I'm going to stay on the ground and have a nice chat with you."

"I can't talk until I get something to eat," said Terrapin.

"I haven't had my lunch yet, either. Let's go find our lunches together," suggested Gray Squirrel.

"Lunch!" exclaimed Terrapin in exasperation. "I haven't had breakfast. And what's more I missed my supper last night."

"Why, Terrapin, you must be starved," said Gray Squirrel. "You poor thing!"

Gray Squirrel spoke so tenderly that Terrapin was

encouraged to tell him about yesterday, his fruitless hike, his sore legs and his hunger.

"Tch, tch, tch," Gray Squirrel sympathized. After a moment of thought he asked, "Are you thirsty, Terrapin?"

Terrapin looked peeved. "Thirsty? Of course I'm thirsty," he snapped. "I belong in water and I haven't been near any for a day or a night. Wouldn't you expect me to be thirsty?"

"I thought you were, that's why I asked," said Gray Squirrel. "I know where there's a tree with ripe persimmons. Ummmmm, the fruit is juicy and watery! The tree's close by. If you could walk a little way, we'd have both food and drink."

Terrapin's eyes brightened. "Persimmons! Where? Oooooo! I love them." Then he looked listless and dejected again and gave Gray Squirrel a disgusted glance. "I might have known you'd offer me food that's on a tree."

"Oh, no, no, Terrapin, you don't understand," protested Gray Squirrel. "I'll go up the tree and throw the persimmons down to you."

Terrapin lifted up creakily. "Ouch!" he screamed and sank down again.

"Try once more. Here, lean on me," said Gray Squirrel stepping close to the shell.

Slowly Terrapin rose on his legs. He screamed, "Ouch!" but not so loudly as before, and limping and groaning he struggled along behind Gray Squirrel. Shortly they met Raccoon who stopped politely and said, "Good morning," and after a little talking hastened down the River Path. Gray Squirrel and Terrapin watched his well-furred body almost dragging on the ground because his legs were short and he ran all crouched up.

"He's a handsome fellow," remarked Gray Squirrel.

Terrapin looked ruefully at his own stubby, hairless tail. "I've always admired 'Coon's long tail with the black and white rings round it," he said.

"There's not another tail in the woods marked that way," said Gray Squirrel. "Have you ever heard the story they tell about Raccoon's tail?"

Terrapin sat down. "A story," he said gratefully. "I'll rest while you tell me."

"It's just a small story," said Gray Squirrel. "A long time ago when the world first was made the animals could not agree about day and night. Some wanted daylight all the time but those who stalked and prowled wanted darkness. A council was called to settle the matter, but everybody argued and made so much noise that the council couldn't make up its mind. My great-great-great-grandmother was there and sat next to

Raccoon. She got awfully tired of all the chatter and when it was her turn to speak, she said:

"'I see that Raccoon has rings on his tail and the circles are evenly divided, first a dark one and then a light one. I think night and day ought to be divided equally in the same way, half the time dark and half the time light.'

"The animals thought she had spoken wisely and so the council decided as my grandmother had spoken. That's why the night is as long as the day."

Terrapin was thoughtful. "It's a good idea," he said. "If you're awake all day, you ought to have just as much time to rest at night." He put down his feet gingerly. "Oooooo! My poor legs! I'll need a couple of nights to rest them and I wouldn't be surprised if I slept through a day too. Ooooo! Believe me, I won't stop crawling until we get to the persimmon tree. It hurts too much to begin again."

Soon they reached the persimmon tree. Gray Squirrel raced up it and out onto a branch where he tapped the fruit with his paws and selected the nicest for Terrapin. "Here you are, Terrapin," he called. "This is the best I've found. Catch!"

Terrapin stood directly beneath Gray Squirrel and his eyes glistened expectantly as he prepared to catch. He saw the red ball dropping and then, when it was almost within his grasp—*it was gone!* Terrapin blinked and his ears detected a crunching sound behind him. There sat Wolf biting into his persimmon.

"Delicious, Terrapin," said Wolf impudently, "and thank you, Gray Squirrel. Drop me down another persimmon."

Gray Squirrel's eyes snapped with anger and he perched indignantly in the tree. "I will not, you greedy Wolf," he said.

Wolf smiled wickedly. Terrapin watched him

silently and thought he didn't care especially for Wolf's smile. There seemed to be a threat back of it.

"So you won't throw me a persimmon," said Wolf threateningly. "Very well, I'll shake you out of the tree."

Gray Squirrel raced to the tip of the branch and leaped to another tree. "You can't shake me out of a tree," he said defiantly. "I'm too fast for you."

Wolf dashed to the tree and began shaking, but Gray Squirrel flew back to the tree he had deserted. Quickly he plucked a persimmon and threw it, calling, "Here, Terrapin, catch!" But Wolf snatched the fruit from the air, and in doing so he rudely knocked Terrapin over on his back.

"Turn me over! Turn me over!" squealed Terrapin, kicking his four feet helplessly in the air. "Turn me over, please!"

Wolf howled with glee and Gray Squirrel gazed down in horror at Terrapin's pathetic plight. Gray Squirrel could do nothing for Terrapin so long as the big Wolf was there.

"Please turn me over!"

"Tell your friend up in the tree to give me some persimmons and then I'll set you right," bargained Wolf.

Gray Squirrel picked a persimmon and dropped it.

"All right, Wolf," he said. "You're a bully just because you're bigger and stronger than Terrapin and I are. Here're your persimmons and I hope they choke you."

Wolf devoured the persimmons as quickly as he caught them. Gray Squirrel threw them hard, as if he would like to hit Wolf, and with each persimmon he pitched, he muttered under his breath, "I wish this one would choke you." Finally his eyes lighted on a very large persimmon and it took as much strength as Gray Squirrel had to pull it off the tree.

"This ought to be big enough to choke Wolf," he said as he called to Wolf, "Here, open your mouth wide. I've got the largest persimmon up here. Open wide!"

Hungrily Wolf stretched his greedy mouth. Dazzling white teeth gleamed along the cruel jaws. With a *swush* the persimmon dropped into them with such force that it did not stop until half-way down Wolf's narrow throat. And there the persimmon wedged itself fast.

"Crumph! Crumph!" coughed Wolf. "Crumph! Crumph! Crumph!" he choked.

But the persimmon stuck.

With delight Gray Squirrel listened to the coughing and choking. Wolf was dancing around in misery, poking first one forepaw and then the other down his throat, but the fruit declined to be dislodged. Gray Squirrel said to himself that he didn't care how much Wolf suffered. But he hoped that Wolf would leave so he could come down out of the tree and put Terrapin back on his feet.

Suddenly, with a quiver of fright, Gray Squirrel saw that Terrapin was in grave danger. Wolf was careening wildly about, with no thought of where he stepped. Several times he had sent the upturned Terrapin spinning like a leaf in the wind. Surely if this kept up Wolf would step on the helpless little beast and crush the life right out of him. But Gray Squirrel could think of nothing to do to save his little friend, lying there on his back kicking his stubby legs in the air and crying out most piteously. He was afraid to venture down the tree with the angry wolf, mad with pain, raging about. Gray Squirrel closed his eyes tightly and put his paws over them so that he might not see poor Terrapin's terrible end.

Thus Gray Squirrel sat in the persimmon tree for what seemed the longest time. Then he heard—or were his ears playing a trick on him? Down went Gray Squirrel's paws. No, he had heard rightly. It *was* Rabbit! Rabbit to the rescue!

Rabbit evidently had watched what was happening

and made up his mind how to act. Wolf was roaring and tearing about most frightfully. Rabbit went up to him and called out his name in a calm, sympathetic voice.

"Wolf, Wolf, oh, Wolf!"

At length Wolf heard.

"You've got a bad cough, Wolf," Rabbit said, as if nothing very serious had happened.

"Crumph! Crumph! Crumph!" said Wolf, but Rabbit's gentle manner had quieted his nerves.

"A big drink of water will stop your choking," said Rabbit. "Why don't you go on down to the River? It's only about a mile. If I were you I'd hurry before that cough gets worse."

"Crumph! Crumph! Crumph!" said Wolf thankfully. Then he seemed ashamed that he had not thought of such a simple thing before and bounded away in the direction of the River.

Gray Squirrel jumped from the persimmon tree and with Rabbit's help Terrapin was turned over. The little shell staggered about dizzily. "Ugh!" said Terrapin, feeling ill. "My insides are all in the wrong place."

"Poor Terrapin!" said Gray Squirrel. "You've had a terrible time. Sit still and I'll get you a persimmon. I didn't give Wolf the biggest one, I saved it for you."

"I'm so hungry," Terrapin said plaintively.

Gray Squirrel climbed the tree and threw an enormous persimmon to Rabbit. Then he rushed back to the ground where he and Rabbit held it up for Terrapin to eat. Terrapin munched his fill, and each bite restored some of his strength. Even his legs felt less sore. When he could eat no more, Gray Squirrel went up the tree once more and dropped some fruit for Rabbit and himself. They sat near Terrapin nibbling at the red balls.

"How'd you happen to come here, Rabbit?" asked Gray Squirrel.

"Wren told me to come. You know how she is, always knows what's going on and what everyone is doing. She's a terrible gossip, but this is one time I'm glad she was poking into what wasn't her business."

"Humph," grunted Terrapin. "Well, she ought to have told you. It was Wren's gossip yesterday started me out on the River Path and got me into all my trouble."

"I was wondering where you were yesterday, Terrapin," said Rabbit. "You missed some fun."

"You wondering where I was!" repeated Terrapin indignantly. "You passed right by me in the path and didn't speak." And Terrapin explained how he had come to be where he was.

"Never you mind, we're going to do something to Wolf," Rabbit comforted him. "He's been very mean to you and I believe we can make him sorry. He's got a garden he's very proud of. I know the beans are ripe because I've been hearing the jar-flies' buzzing."

"Beans!" exclaimed Gray Squirrel. "I adore them."

"Beans!" exclaimed Terrapin sorrowfully. "I love 'em, but I'm too full of persimmon to eat any."

"Well, I've got an idea," said Rabbit. "Let's go to sleep now and tonight we'll go prowling."

"But I don't prowl," said Gray Squirrel.

"I don't prowl," said Terrapin.

"Neither do I prowl," said Rabbit, "but I thought I'd like to try it once. We'll prowl in Wolf's garden where there're beans."

"Ummmmm," said Terrapin. "It might be fun to prowl once."

"All right," agreed Gray Squirrel.

And so they all lay down side by side, closed their eyes and took a nap in the shade beneath the persimmon tree.

Chapter XII

The Rescue of Rabbit

Rabbit, Terrapin and Gray Squirrel woke up at dusk with an appetite for beans.

"I don't know where Wolf lives," said Gray Squirrel.

"I know," said Rabbit.

"Then, let's start," said Gray Squirrel.

He and Rabbit started but after taking a few steps they noiced that Terrapin was not following.

"Come on, Terrapin," called Gray Squirrel.

"I'm not going," said Terrapin.

"What!" exclaimed Rabbit in surprise.

"I'm not going," repeated Terrapin.

"Why?" asked Gray Squirrel.

Terrapin hesitated before saying, "I'm tired," and his hesitation made Rabbit look at him suspiciously.

"Now, what's the matter with you?" Rabbit asked impatiently.

"Well, Rabbit, I like beans, but I don't like Wolf," Terrapin simpered. "I'd rather not go near him."

"Oh, come on, Terrapin," urged Rabbit. "We won't let anything happen to you. We'll keep Wolf from getting near you."

Then Terrapin said he was lame, and then he wasn't hungry, and his foot hurt, and he didn't see well at night, but in spite of all these things Rabbit and Gray Squirrel persuaded him to go along. They promised him lots of fun.

The three of them walked through the dark woods boasting what big appetites they had.

"I'm going to eat beans and squash—rows of 'em," said Gray Squirrel.

"I hope Wolf has enough lettuce," said Rabbit. "I'll be satisfied with a whole row."

"I just want beans—all the beans Wolf has," said Terrapin.

But when they came almost face to face with the garden, the talking ceased. They suddenly lost their appetites. Rabbit broke the silence.

"I wonder if, by any chance, Wolf could have stayed home tonight," he said.

"I shouldn't be surprised," said Gray Squirrel. "He's got four legs and any one of them might have gone lame and kept him from prowling."

"Oooooo!" Terrapin shivered. "Let's go home before we get into trouble. I'm sure Wolf is waiting for us in his garden. Let's go! I'm scared."

"I don't feel like eating. Probably had too many persimmons at lunchtime," said Gray Squirrel. "I'd just as soon come back another time."

"I'm not especially hungry, either," said Rabbit. "We really oughtn't to bother if we're not hungry. Another time will be better."

"Oooooo," said Terrapin. "Let's go and never come back."

So they turned around and headed for their homes. But Rabbit was not exactly satisfied to give up a thing that had promised to be so much fun.

"I'll tell you what I'll do," he said, halting. "I'll slip quietly into Wolf's garden, nose around and see if he's there. You wait here and I'll come back and let you know."

Gray Squirrel and Terrapin waited, jumping at the slightest sound. Rabbit's going made them feel more lonely and more scary. The dark shadows in the woods looked giant-like and menacing. They imagined all sorts of things lurking there. Way off in the forest they heard a noise that resembled first a sigh and then a muffled cracking of twigs. Terrapin leaned closer to Gray Squirrel.

"What's that?" he whispered.

But Gray Squirrel could reassure him. "Nothing to be afraid of, Terrapin. Haven't you ever heard that sound before? That's the forest growing. They say it's a growing pain, but I don't believe it actually hurts."

Rabbit came bounding back. Breathlessly he said that Wolf had gone prowling and the garden was chockful of vegetables. "Hurry, I can't wait to begin eating. I'm terribly hungry."

"I hope there's enough for the three of us," said Gray Squirrel. "This long walk has given me an appetite, too."

Terrapin crawled into the garden and stopped before the peas. It was the first time he had ever seen peas.

"Shell yourself some peas," said Rabbit.

Terrapin looked at the long green pods Rabbit pointed to and then he twisted his neck and looked at his own shell. "Shell them?" he inquired, not understanding.

"Yes," said Rabbit tearing off a lettuce leaf and stuffing it into his mouth. "You don't want to eat the shell."

"Don't I?" asked Terrapin.

"Of course not," said Rabbit.

Uncertainly Terrapin stripped a shell from the vine, shoved it into the corner of his jaw and began to chew. He didn't like the tough outside, but inside was something soft with a sweet flavor.

"Not that way," said Rabbit taking the shell from his mouth. "You take peas out of their pods—like this." And Rabbit snapped open the shell and gave Terrapin the half-dozen small green balls within. "Eat these," he said and picking another shell from the vine, Rabbit opened it. "They call 'em laughing peas, Terrapin, because, look, when I tear them open they crackle as if they were laughing. See?"

Terrapin's mouth was full of the sweet little balls. He swallowed and asked, "Rabbit, have I got green peas inside my shell?"

Rabbit laughed. "Silly Terrapin!" he said. "You'll have green peas inside your shell before the night is over."

A new and fascinating pursuit was this shelling of the laughing peas. And "pursuit" it was in truth for Terrapin. Holding a shell with his forepaw, he opened it by drawing it over the horny corner of his mouth and out rolled the peas in every direction with Terrapin crawling this way and that to pick them up. By the time Terrapin had eaten his fill he was exhausted from the chase.

Rabbit and Gray Squirrel ate their fill too, although not half so many rows as they said they would, and began binding up bundles of vegetables to take home with them.

"Won't Wolf be terribly mad?" said Gray Squirrel, chuckling.

"I hate to go away without seeing how mad he gets, but I think we had better leave," said Rabbit.

After the three animals had departed Wolf returned just at daybreak. His anger was, indeed, worth seeing. He tore about the garden searching in every corner and under every bush, howling, "Where's the thief? Where's the thief? I'll find him! I'll catch him!"

The next few days Wolf spent making a scarecrow to resemble himself. Wolf simply had to go prowling nights and he thought that, if he left the scarecrow in the garden while he was away, a thief would be deceived into thinking it was really Wolf and would keep out. Wolf molded the scarecrow of clay and when it was standing like a statue in his garden he made several trips into the woods, collecting the sticky gum from the barks of pine trees. He coated the scarecrow all over with the gum to keep the moisture in the clay. If the sun dried it out, the clay wolf would crumble and fall apart.

For a week after the scarecrow was set up, Wolf

was happy to find that no one invaded his garden. He believed the scarecrow was a success and was really scaring off thieves and so Wolf walked proudly among his vegetables thinking he had devised an exceedingly clever scheme for their protection.

The truth of the matter was, of course, that during this time Rabbit, Gray Squirrel and Terrapin were merrily feasting on the loot they had carried away. When the last lettuce leaf was gone, they found it a hardship to strike out into the woods once more and find their next meal. On Wolf's vegetables they had grown plump and lazy. After a day of food-searching, Rabbit said he wasn't going to bother again.

"I can't see why I should take this trouble when Wolf has a garden filled with vegetables," he argued. "Besides there's nothing in the woods to compare in quality. Tonight I shall prowl and get me another supply of food."

"I wouldn't, Rabbit," advised Gray Squirrel. "Wolf's too smart to let you steal his vegetables a second time. I'll bet he's rigged up some sort of trap by now."

"Oooo, please don't go again, Rabbit," begged Terrapin.

Rabbit laughed at their fears. "I'm as smart as Wolf," he said. "He'll not catch me."

At twilight Rabbit set out, promising to bring back a good meal for all. Gray Squirrel ran up a tree and went to bed and Terrapin shoved himself into Rabbit's burrow at the bottom of the tree. He dropped off to sleep right away and sometime later woke with a start. He felt the light outside; it must be dawn. Terrapin poked his way out of the burrow. The light was moonlight, but Terrapin was just as wide awake as if it had been sunlight. Moreover, he was hungry. There weren't any vegetables and this meant that Rabbit had not returned.

For a time Terrapin paced back and forth before the burrow, listening for a sound of Rabbit. It was awfully quiet, although Terrapin thought he could see something moving among the dark shadows of the trees. When he looked hard, the movement ceased, but when he turned his back he felt it begin again.

"If Rabbit were here, he could tell me for sure whether anything was hiding there," Terrapin thought. He wished Rabbit would come. When he was around, everything that was wrong seemed to straighten itself and get right. Like the time the big rock fell on Terrapin's back. Rabbit had come to rescue him and he fixed up the back right.

"Oh, dear, maybe Rabbit is in trouble and I ought to go rescue him," said Terrapin. "Maybe Wolf has caught him. I've got to rescue Rabbit."

In his excitement Terrapin began to crawl round and round the tree and say he had to rescue Rabbit. After about the sixth time around, he couldn't help seeing that although he was breathless from the haste of his crawling, still the rescue of Rabbit had got exactly nowhere.

"Gray Squirrel! Gray Squirrel!" he shouted frantically.

Gray Squirrel slid down the tree. "What's the matter?" he asked.

"We've got to rescue Rabbit," said Terrapin. "There're no vegetables. He isn't back yet."

The Rescue of Rabbit

Gray Squirrel looked worried. After all it was late and Rabbit should have returned.

"Something must have happened to him," said Gray Squirrel. "Dear me, I wish he had taken my advice and not gone. Wolf is cunning. Yes, Terrapin, we'll have to try to rescue Rabbit."

So the two animals fared forth in the moonlight, but before they had gone far Gray Squirrel suggested that he race ahead and leave Terrapin to follow.

"That's a good idea," Terrapin agreed.

Gray Squirrel was correct in his surmise. Something *had* happened to Rabbit, something that not even Wolf had counted on when he modeled his scarecrow.

Over-confident from the success of his first night of prowling, Rabbit had boldly leaped into the garden without first taking a quiet look around. And he found himself confronted by the scarecrow. It fooled Rabbit.

"G-g-g-good evening, Wolf," he stammered, endeavoring to hide his surprise.

The scarecrow was silent which seemed like a very bad sign to Rabbit. "Wolf must be awfully mad," he thought, and so he tried carrying on a very friendly conversation.

"Your garden keeps you working late," Rabbit said pleasantly. "Plenty of weeds this time of year. I think we're going to have rain. My nose itches—that's always a sign of rain."

There was no response and Rabbit proceeded with his conversation. He said to himself. "If I ask Wolf a question, he'll have to answer."

And so he tried this: "Wolf, did you find the River all right the other day when you were choking on the persimmon?"

No answer, but Rabbit thought perhaps he knew the reason. "Is the persimmon still in your throat?" he asked sympathetically.

Still no answer. Rabbit then was sure the fruit was in Wolf's throat and with a forepaw reached out to feel for the lump. *And his paw stuck fast to the dark figure.*

"Let me go!" he screamed, pulling desperately to release himself. The gum held fast. In panic Rabbit reached out with his other forepaw to brace himself for a good yank and thoughtlessly shoved it against the scarecrow. The second paw stuck.

"Let me go!" Rabbit cried. "Help! Help! Help! I'm caught!"

In no time he wore himself out screaming and pulling and finally just stood and whimpered. He had plenty of time for investigation and soon learned he was sticking to a scarecrow and not to Wolf at all. Not

The Rescue of Rabbit 199

that this really made a great deal of difference. Rabbit realized he was trapped and knew that when Wolf got back from prowling a dreadful punishment would be his. Wolf was never known to be kind. Rabbit sobbed wildly.

And he was sobbing when Gray Squirrel crept into the garden.

"Rabbit, what *is* the matter?" asked Gray Squirrel.

Rabbit told him and by the light of the moon showed how he was held a prisoner.

"Poor Rabbit," said Gray Squirrel and rubbed the captive's shoulders which ached from the pulling and yanking.

"Ouch!" Rabbit squealed frequently, for his paws around Rabbit's waist and together they tugged and heaved and struggled, but without avail.

"Ouch!" Rabbit squealed frequently, for his paws were sore.

"Let's try once more," encouraged Gray Squirrel.

But it was no use. The gum stretched a little bit, but would not let go of Rabbit.

"What am I to do?" Rabbit asked tearfully.

Gray Squirrel studied the wolf scarecrow. "I can't do anything for you, but I might try to find some big animal to help us," he said.

"Oh, do hurry and bring a big, *big* animal," pleaded

Rabbit. "Wolf will be back soon. He'll probably beat me."

Gray Squirrel rushed over the path, but met no one until he came upon Terrapin, creeping to Rabbit's rescue. Terrapin could hardly help in pulling Rabbit away from the scarecrow, but still and all when he heard how his friend had been trapped Terrapin was a big help.

"Hurry down this path," said Terrapin to Gray Squirrel. "I passed Brown Bear not long since."

Terrapin hastened toward Wolf's garden and Gray Squirrel flew off in the opposite direction, but not many minutes later he returned with Brown Bear at his side. Overtaking Terrapin they entered Wolf's garden. The big bear stumped solemnly around the scarecrow, looking it over carefully, while the three small animals watched him in silent hope.

"Rabbit, you're good and stuck," said Brown Bear.

"Yes, we know that," replied Terrapin. "You unstick him."

Again Brown Bear stumped around the scarecrow, pausing after nearly every step to sway thoughtfully from side to side. "I can separate you from this thing," he said at last, "but it's going to hurt."

A sob caught Rabbit's breath. "Just free me, I won't mind the hurt," he said.

Brown Bear lumbered over to the grapevine bordering the garden and tore off a long rope of it. He wrapped the vine around the scarecrow like a lasso. He ordered Gray Squirrel to stand behind Rabbit and clasp him around the waist and Terrapin to clasp Gray Squirrel in the same manner.

"When I say 'Ready, go!' you two pull Rabbit and I'll pull the scarecrow," said Brown Bear. "And, Rabbit, you pull too and pull your hardest. Are you ready? All right—ready, *go!*"

With the three small animals pulling one way and Brown Bear pulling the other the gum beneath Rabbit's paws began to stretch like soft, warm taffy candy. First it made a thick rope, then, a thinner one, then a fine thread and then it broke, sending Terrapin, Gray Squirrel and Rabbit sprawling in one direction and Brown Bear in the other.

"Owwww!" screamed Rabbit in pain.

"Ha! Ha! Ha!" laughed Gray Squirrel and Terrapin in a tangled heap a little way from Rabbit.

Brown Bear lay on the ground with chuckles shaking his great body over which his coat of fur fit loosely as if it were too large for him.

Rabbit was the first to get up and the moment he stood on his feet he again screamed, "Owww!" His forepaws were so sore and besides lumps of gum clung to his pads. Standing or walking felt as if he were treading on stones.

"Thank you, Brown Bear," he said, "and thank you, Gray Squirrel and Terrapin. You've rescued me."

"I think we ought to be going," said Gray Squirrel. "It's almost dawn and Wolf will soon be home."

Brown Bear rubbed the back of his neck with one of his paws and glanced at the garden. "Wolf certainly has a fine lot of vegetables," he said. "They make me hungry. Wolf has put us all to a lot of trouble tonight. I think he should be made to pay. Let's gather some of his vegetables and take them into the woods for a breakfast-picnic."

"A good idea," said Rabbit. "I'm hungry after all the yelling I did."

"The excitement has given me an appetite, too," said Gray Squirrel.

"I'd love to shell some peas," said Terrapin.

The four worked busily selecting and piling up a mound of vegetables. Brown Bear loaded Rabbit's forearms with greens. "Rabbit, I'll carry you on my shoulder," he said. "You're too lame to walk." He looked at the diminutive Terrapin who was shelling and eating peas. "Terrapin," he added, "if I carry you on my other shoulder, then you can carry some peas." Brown Bear looked at Gray Squirrel, smiled and said, "There's nothing wrong with you, Gray Squirrel, so you'll have to walk."

They were a jolly little party as they swung along the path, chattering and laughing and talking expectantly of the breakfast-picnic. Brown Bear started singing in his rich bass voice. The three small animals sang with him, but soon gave up because his voice was so powerful that it drowned out theirs.

Suddenly Gray Squirrel gave an alarmed gasp and an expression of terror swept over his face. Brown Bear abruptly ceased his singing.

"What is it?" asked Rabbit.

"Wolf," said Gray Squirrel. "Listen."

The animals listened. The morning was so windless and still that one could have heard a leaf fall. The first beams of day were peeping through the treetops to send away the shadows of night to their Day Home in the great caves of the mountain.

"Listen," repeated Gray Squirrel in a whisper.

And surely enough there came to the ears of the four animals the regular *jog, jog, jog* of Wolf's tread coming toward them in the path. No animal except Wolf made this sound. He was returning home after his usual all-night prowl.

"Quick," said Brown Bear, who could move his great, clumsy-looking body with surprising swiftness when he had to. With Rabbit perched on one shoulder and Terrapin on the other, the bear slipped from the trail into the woods, Gray Squirrel running behind him. A great rock offered a place to hide and Brown Bear stepped behind it but as he did so his foot caught in a root and sent him sprawling. Terrapin, Rabbit and all the vegetables they were carrying went into a heap.

This mishap made a great noise in the stillness of the early morning. The jog, jog of Wolf's feet stopped. He had heard, and was listening. But Wolf was tired from his long prowl, and sleepy. He wanted to get home. Jog, jog. Here he came again.

The animals lay very still. Wolf passed them by without so much as glancing right or left.

Brown Bear heaved a tremendous sigh. Then he looked at Rabbit and all four of them burst out laughing and they laughed until the tears ran down their faces.

At last Brown Bear was able to stop and he said, "Since we're here and our vegetables are already unpacked, let's have breakfast in this spot."

They ate their fill, and afterward when they were talking about Rabbit's gum-covered paws, Brown Bear told them about his own feet.

"Did you notice that I wear my feet wrong?" he

The Rescue of Rabbit 205

asked. "My left foot is my right and my right is my left."

Of course the animals had noticed that all bears, including Black Bear, their leader, had feet like that. But none had ever dared to ask why. It would not have been polite.

"Yes," said Gray Squirrel, "I've noticed. Don't you find walking uncomfortable?"

"No, I'm used to it," replied Brown Bear. "I've never had any other kind of feet. We bears have had mixed-up feet ever since our great-great-great-grandfather's day. That was during the time when the animals who preferred the day wanted day all the time and the animals who preferred the night wanted night all the time. They decided to settle the matter by playing a game of hide-the-stone. At dusk the animals who wore them took off their moccasins—in those days a number of the animals wore slippers because their feet were new and tender—and placed them top-side down in a long row. Then they hid their eyes while other animals placed small stones under some of the moccasins. The game was for the players to guess whether a moccasin had a stone under it or not. The side that guessed where most of the stones were hidden was the winner.

"The game began, but right away Magpie and Quail, who love the light, cheated. They have sharp eyes and they peeked and told the other day animals where to look for the stones. After that they had to start the game all over again. The animals played far into the night, losing all track of time. When Magpie impatiently began her song of the morning, the score was a tie. Nothing had been settled. The night players looked up at the dawn lighting the sky and rushed wildly after their moccasins. My great-great-great-grandfather was in such a hurry to get home before the Sun was up that he put his moccasins on the wrong feet and ever since the bears' feet have been—well, on the wrong foot.

"And that's how it came about. But gracious me! The Sun is climbing into the sky vault now. I've got to get home myself."

Brown Bear stood up on his "wrong feet," yawned and stretched. "Good-by," he said, "and I hope we'll have a breakfast-picnic some other morning. Maybe we can get Wolf to give us some greens from his garden."

Gray Squirrel and Rabbit laughed. Terrapin was quiet because—he had gone to sleep in his shell.

"Terrapin's had a tiring night," said Gray Squirrel. "He'll never make a prowler."

"And neither will I," said Rabbit. "After this experience I never want to prowl again."

"That's too bad," said Brown Bear. "We can't meet often if you don't prowl. But I must be going. Good-by, again."

"Good-by and many thanks for rescuing me," said Rabbit.

With long strides Brown Bear swung into the path and was gone.

Rabbit rubbed his sticky paws. "They hurt awfully," he said. "I can't walk a step. I'm going to lie down and go to sleep beside Terrapin."

Gray Squirrel yawned. "I'm too sleepy to bother with going home," he said. "I'll sleep on the other side of Terrapin."

Before the Sun had climbed very far that morning the three tired little animals were sound asleep in a friendly heap.

Chapter XIII

Rabbit is banished to the island . . . .

Rabbit could not walk home for a week and so Gray Squirrel and Terrapin stayed with him in the woods, keeping him company and bringing him his meals. After the long period of idleness, Rabbit was bursting with energy. He was so energetic, in fact, that when he was well at last he began running about with Deer, the fleetest animal in the woods.

It was really difficult for Rabbit to run with Deer. Rabbit was good on short runs and leaps, but Deer was a distance runner and Rabbit trailed after him puffing and gasping for breath almost as badly as Terrapin did when he tried to keep up with Rabbit. But Rabbit was too ambitious to give up and admit that Deer outran him. Each time he caught up with Deer he invented a lengthy story to explain his delay. He had stopped to look at something, or he had met a friend, or else he had gone to investigate a noise.

Deer would smile at his excuses, but Rabbit had the feeling that his new-found companion did not altogether believe him. This annoyed Rabbit and so he strove all the more in his efforts to run faster and longer. The queer side of his story-telling was that even if he did not succeed in convincing Deer, Rabbit began to believe in some of his excuses himself! And, as might be expected, this error presently had him involved in a deal of trouble.

Late one afternoon Deer and Rabbit were sitting in the woods with several of their friends when Deer suddenly got to his feet, ran a few steps and leaped high over a fallen tree. He turned, ran back and jumped again, for the sheer joy of sailing high through the air. His leaps were graceful and the animals looked on admiringly.

"What a marvelous runner Deer is," observed Brown Bear. "He is the swiftest of all animals. Look—look at him fly over that log! Whew!"

Rabbit twisted his little body enviously. Before he knew what he was saying, he bragged, "I can run as fast as Deer, and leap as high too."

The animals tittered. "Ho! Ho! You can run as fast as deer. Ho! Ho! That's a good one," scoffed Brown Bear.

"I can too run as fast," Rabbit repeated with heat.

"All right, get up and run," invited Brown Bear indifferently.

"Not here," said Rabbit.

"Oh, not here. I guess you know you'd be licked," said Brown Bear.

"I guess I wouldn't be licked," flung back Rabbit. "I'm just not prepared to run this afternoon."

"Whoever heard of being prepared to run?" questioned Brown Bear. "Didn't you see Deer get up and run and leap? *He* wasn't prepared. What you mean is you were bragging and now you'd like to back out without making good your boast."

Rabbit himself could not have stated the actual truth of the case more clearly. Since the argument began he had been wishing—oh, how he had been wishing!—that he had kept his mouth tight shut. Of course, Deer could outrace him, but Brown Bear's taunts had the effect of drawing him on to more extravagant talk.

"Back out!" Rabbit repeated in a tone of deep offense. "I wouldn't think of it. I'm going to have a race with Deer, but it'll be a big race with everybody invited to attend." That, thought Rabbit, most certainly would make Brown Bear think him sincere and put a stop to his mocking.

Brown Bear looked at the smaller animal and coolly

asked, "Do you think anyone will be interested in attending such a race?"

Rabbit ignored his sarcasm and proceeded volubly with his plans. "It'll be a big event," he said importantly. "We'll run over a long course so Deer will really have a chance. For myself—long or short—it doesn't matter. I'll see Black Bear immediately and have him set the day. Naturally he'll want to be the judge. I must be going now. See you soon. Goodby."

With all the speed his legs could command, Rabbit dashed off. He thought he left behind him an impression that he was a racer and eager beyond a doubt to match his sturdy legs against Deer's. But once away from Brown Bear he had no intention of finding Black Bear. If he should have the misfortune soon to meet Brown Bear accidentally he could say that Black Bear had been away on a journey and was unable to make any plans for the race. Thus he hoped to keep putting off the race until Brown Bear and the other animals would eventually forget all about his boasting.

Rabbit went back to Terrapin and Gray Squirrel and found contentment in their slower-paced company. The days passed pleasantly, even though Rabbit stayed close to home, lest he encounter Brown Bear. When he thought the animals had had time to forget, he be-

Rabbit Is Banished to the Island 213

gan roaming once more and the first beast he met was Brown Bear whose memory was very, very good.

"What about the race with Deer?" he asked.

"Well, er—er—uh—er—it's—er—this way," Rabbit faltered. "Black Bear's been on a long trip and I haven't seen him yet."

"That's funny, I saw him yesterday and he didn't mention he'd been traveling," said Brown Bear.

"It was a secret trip," fibbed Rabbit.

Brown Bear stared straight into Rabbit's eyes and tightening his mouth grimly said, "Anyway, Black Bear is not traveling now and he wants to see you. He'd like for you to race Deer and Deer is ready for the contest."

Having delivered this upsetting message, Brown Bear walked away without another word, not even good-by. Inside Rabbit was upheaval and confusion. He kicked the ground angrily and called himself an idiot. There was nothing he could do now. A summons from Black Bear was a command and so with spirits low Rabbit betook himself to the leader of the animals.

He found that Black Bear was delighted with the idea of a race with Deer and had practically completed all the arrangements. All that was left for Rabbit to do was to name the day. Rabbit named a distant day, hoping something would turn up meanwhile to prevent the race and save him from disgrace. He was made more miserable still when Black Bear showed him the prize for the winner. It was a crown which Black Bear called antlers. The antlers resembled a small branching tree without leaves and Rabbit admired their graceful, rigid lines. He had never seen anything like antlers before in Atagahi. Black Bear permitted him to put them on his head for a moment. Rabbit thought he looked very handsome and distinguished wearing antlers and his heart ached at the thought that such a prize was out of his reach.

He went back to his burrow and remained inside for several days. No longer was he concerned about the race he was bound to lose, but the thought of the antlers going to Deer made him moody and ill. When he went out for food—and this was not very often because he had lost his appetite—he walked slowly and drearily. He was thinking and thinking of ways to get possession of the antlers, but no really worthwhile idea presented itself.

The day before the race Rabbit walked with grave face and melancholy tread over the race-course. Tomorrow he would see the antlers won by Deer and the thought made his heart heavy. Black Bear saw the crestfallen little figure trudging along looking sadly at his toes. He shook his head. "That Rabbit," said the leader of the animals to himself. "I don't know what I'll ever do with him. He's one of my favorite subjects. He tickles me with lots of his mischief, but he's got to learn not to brag. It'll serve him right to lose this race tomorrow. The nerve of him, thinking he can run as fast and leap as well as Deer!"

When Rabbit returned from the race-course, he was running and leaping, not as high as Deer of course, but his drooping spirits had left him and an idea for winning the antlers lifted him into a seventh heaven. He had had a tussle with his conscience before actually deciding to use the idea because it required some cheating, but the memory of the antlers made him willing to risk a punishment for the sake of gaining them.

The morning of the race he went early to the race-course, prancing and skipping with light, gay steps. Black Bear was already on hand, busy with last-minute arranging.

"Good morning," said Rabbit cheerily.

The leader of the animals looked at him quizzically. This suddenly acquired good humor puzzled Black Bear. "Now what's he up to?" was the question that popped immediately into Black Bear's head, but he replied, "Good morning," genially, and Rabbit had no inkling of the suspicions in his mind.

"I thought I'd look over the race-course again," said Rabbit casually.

"Go right ahead," said Black Bear.

Rabbit pranced off, not stopping until well out of Black Bear's sight. At this point the race path ran straight through tall grass and brush that towered high on each side like walls. On his trip of inspection the day before Rabbit had found a loose bush which Beaver, with his sharp teeth, had nipped off and removed from the path, to clear it for the racers. Straining every muscle Rabbit dragged the bush back into the race-course, making a barrier right across it. Then, branching off to the right Rabbit smoothed a false path through the tall green snake-grass. Rabbit extended this path for quite a way, until it reached a dense thicket of brush. That, he thought, would be far enough.

By all this exertion Rabbit hoped to deceive Deer into believing that the false path through the grass was the race-course. In this way he hoped to send Deer astray and get him entangled in the brush thicket. By the time Deer discovered his mistake Rabbit expected to be so far ahead on the race path as to win the contest.

It was hard work trampling down the tough grass which would bend but not break. But Rabbit worked with a will, for he wanted those antlers. So intent was he on his labor that he lost track of the time, and Black Bear came to see what was keeping him. Black Bear crept up quietly and Rabbit was not warned that he was near until he spoke.

"Well, Rabbit, I see you're planning to win this race," he said.

Rabbit's heart turned over and jumped into his throat where it lay cramped and aching. He couldn't say a word.

"I'm ashamed of you," said Black Bear. "You meant to cheat. Once I thought I had taught you not to cheat, but I suppose my punishment was not severe enough."

Rabbit was ashamed, now that he was caught. His head dropped onto his chest and he couldn't look at Black Bear. Neither could he talk. But as he had to do something he sat and stared at his left hind foot. Tears welled up into his eyes. They got bigger and bigger. Looking through these tears Rabbit saw his foot seem to swell up into a great misshapen mass. Suddenly the mass burst. Rabbit let out a little cry.

"Oh, my foot."

But nothing had happened to his foot. Merely the tears that Rabbit was looking through had burst and splashed to the ground.

"You've lost the race by default," said Black Bear

sternly. "I shall give the antlers to Deer. And *you*"—Black Bear knit his brows most fearfully as he pondered Rabbit's fate—"and *you* will go to the Island!"

Rabbit lifted his eyes in terror. "Not the Island!" he begged. "Please, Black Bear, don't send me there. Punish me any other way, but not the Island. The grubworms live on the Island."

"You shall go and live with the grubworms," said Black Bear firmly.

"Ooohh!" sobbed Rabbit. "I don't like grubworms and I don't like all the water around the Island."

"I don't like cheaters," said Black Bear grimly.

Rabbit closed his eyes and a shudder ran through his body as he pictured his exile among the grubworms on an island entirely surrounded by water. Ugh! Hopefully he sought a small measure of consolation. "How long will I stay on the Island?" he asked.

"A long time," Black Bear replied unfeelingly.

Black Bear led Rabbit back to where the race with Deer was to have started. The crowd had assembled and, with his head bowed in shame, Rabbit heard the leader of the animals announce that the race was off because Rabbit had been discovered in a trick to cheat Deer. The animals booed and shook angry fists in Rabbit's direction. Then Black Bear, with a tribute to Deer's fleetness and honesty, awarded the antlers. The

Rabbit Is Banished to the Island 219

animals shrilled their applause as the prize was fitted to Deer's head and even Rabbit had to admit, although grudgingly, that Deer wore his new crown becomingly. Deer proudly walked a few steps and then the antlers

lost their balance and slipped sidewise. The crowd laughed loudly with amusement and Deer was quite flustered for a moment.

Rabbit's nose twitched with disapproval. He told himself that nothing of the sort would have happened if he had won the antlers. But, getting used to them must have been a little difficult because Deer, who loved grace above anyone, nearly lost his crown half a dozen times before he could stalk among his friends and receive their congratulations.

"Come along, Rabbit," said Black Bear.

Nobody called out good-by as Rabbit marched off with Black Bear on one side of him and Brown Bear on the other. Silently the three made their way to the landing on the River where the raft to ferry exiles across to the Island was kept.

Rabbit gazed at the water with bitter hate. This was what he must look at while he was prisoner, water and grubworms. Ugh! And not a moment would he be able to get away from the sound of rushing, splashing water. Ugh!

"Brown Bear will take you over on the raft," said Black Bear, "and then he'll come back and sit guard here. This is the narrowest part of the River and I'll keep a guard to see that you do not escape by swimming. Brown Bear, I'll send another animal to relieve you after a few hours."

Rabbit stepped fearfully onto the swaying raft. He could have assured Black Bear he would never try to escape, if it meant he had to swim, but he was too downcast to speak. He had settled himself as best he could in the center of the raft when Brown Bear shuffled aboard and his weight made waves in the River, spattering Rabbit's fur with spray. This was

Rabbit Is Banished to the Island

drowning, thought Rabbit, and in fright covered his face with his forepaws. If he were going to drown at least he could spare himself the sight of the water.

Drowning apparently took a long time. When he could no longer stand the suspense, Rabbit lowered his paws. The raft was bumping the Island. He had crossed the River without drowning, strange to say. Brown Bear picked Rabbit up by the back of his neck, dropped him on shore, and without a word started paddling back to the mainland. Rabbit was utterly alone. He sat down where he was and cried. Something tickled his toes. Cabbages and lettuce leaves! It was a grubworm underfoot. In disgust Rabbit jumped up and darted away.

Several days later Deer was on guard at the raft landing when he looked over the water and saw Terrapin's knob of a head pointed straight for the Island.

"Hey, you!" shouted Deer. "Come back! You're not allowed on the Island. Rabbit can't have visitors."

Terrapin turned and stopped swimming. "Who, me?" he asked.

"Yes, you. Come here."

Terrapin kicked his short legs angrily in the River. He had blundered because he was careless. "Ooooo," he growled, swimming toward Deer. "I'm plain stupid. I can't do anything right. If I had any sense

I'd have ducked my head way back there and swam to the Island under water."

Terrapin had not been among the throng of animals who booed Rabbit and would not tell him good-by. When he arrived at the race-course late, as might be expected, Rabbit had been led away by Black Bear and Brown Bear. As soon as he heard of Rabbit's banishment, he had set out for the Island.

"Poor Rabbit, he must feel awful," said Terrapin. "How he hates water! And grubworms! And he's really not so bad. It seems to me everybody has forgotten the nice things he did. Well, he fixed my back and I'm still grateful. I'm going to the Island to keep him company. I like water and maybe I can show Rabbit how to enjoy it."

Crawling and swimming, it had taken Terrapin two days to get as far as he did before Deer spied him.

"Why, Terrapin, I never expected to meet you so far from your home," Deer greeted him as he climbed onto the river bank.

Terrapin shook the water from his shell. "I never expected to get so far myself. Whew! Roaming is tiresome."

"Not half as tiresome as sitting around doing guard duty," said Deer. "I'm almost as much of a prisoner as Rabbit."

Terrapin looked up with bright eyes. "You go away and I'll be guard for a while," he urged eagerly.

Deer smiled. "Terrapin, you're trying to get me to go away so Rabbit can make his escape, I do believe," he said.

Terrapin's mouth opened in surprise. "Oh, you're too smart, Deer. I'm not smart enough to do anything, I guess. Maybe I'm too small. If I were bigger I might do big things. I came all the way down the River to help Rabbit and now that I'm here I feel so small and helpless and useless."

"You couldn't do anything for Rabbit if you were bigger," said Deer. "He has to be punished for cheating. It's our duty to see that he learns his lesson."

"Tch, tch," said Terrapin. "Duty hasn't anything to do with it. If I were as big a deer as you are I'd simply push you out of the way."

"Why, Terrapin, I don't believe you could be so rude," Deer joked.

"Tch, tch! I'd push you out of the way in a minute, if I thought I could."

Deer pretended a shiver of fear. "Oh, Terrapin, I'm scared of you!"

"Bah!" exclaimed Terrapin indignantly. "You're not fooling me, Deer. You're teasing me, but you wouldn't tease if I were big. You'd treat me with respect because you'd be afraid to do anything else. That's why I'm Rabbit's friend and I'd do anything to rescue him. He's kind and polite to me even if I am littler and can't move fast."

"But if you had something that Rabbit wanted he'd try to cheat you out of it," said Deer. "He's kind and polite to you because he doesn't want to take anything from you. I'd never trust him again."

"He's my friend and I'll trust him," said Terrapin hotly.

Also he glared wrathfully. How he wished, right this moment, he were bigger! He'd punch Deer on his nose. He needn't be so superior now that he had antlers. Talking like that, just because Terrapin was little.

Terrapin crawled furiously toward the water. He didn't know where he was going, but he wasn't going to stay and have Deer twitting him in this unfeeling fashion. At the River's edge he paused and, pulling his tiny face into the worst possible sneer, said, "Anyway, when Rabbit tricks someone, he doesn't pick out a small animal. He chooses a great big animal, twenty times his size—like you!"

Deer laughed merrily at Terrapin's serious behavior. "Terrapin, please, you're hurting my pride." Then he felt that perhaps he had gone a little too far with his fun, and so he said appeasingly, "Anyway you're just as ambitious as Rabbit. Didn't you try to trick me a while ago, and I'm at least forty times your size. Next thing I know you'll be bobbing up here and challenging me to a race!"

Deer was teasing again and so Terrapin summoned back his sneer. "Well, maybe I will challenge you to a race," he said defiantly.

Deer had to laugh. "That's the spirit, Terrapin. And when you win I'll go to Black Bear and plead with him to release your dear friend Rabbit."

"Bah!" spat Terrapin and plopped into the River where he could hear no more of Deer's ridicule.

Not until he had gone around a bend and was well out of hearing did Terrapin come up for air. His swim had refreshed him and somewhat cooled his temper. His snubby nose bumped softly against the long stem of something. He looked up; the stem belonged to a feathery body. It was Heron, in wading as usual.

"How do you do, Heron?" Terrapin said.

"Not so well," Heron replied sadly. "The fishing is poor."

Terrapin put his head on the side and observed, "I can't say that I blame the fish for staying away from you."

"But I must eat to live, which really doesn't interfere in any way with the habits of fish," said Heron. "Fish live to be eaten. As you see, the problem works out rather nicely for both of us."

With a frown Terrapin thought the matter over. "No," he disagreed, "it's bad for the fish. If they're eaten they don't live."

Heron shook his head slowly, with assurance. "You haven't gone to the heart of the matter, Terrapin. This is it. If the fish live to be eaten and I eat to live and if I am not eating and the fish are not being eaten, then neither fish nor I will live. You see?"

Terrapin blinked his eyes and shook his head violently. His brain was all in a whirl. Heron had spoken such a lot of words. The animals said Heron was a wise old bird and so, although Terrapin did not "see," he said, "Uh-huh," much perplexed.

Still trying to collect his thoughts, Terrapin remarked solemnly, "I'm looking for a good idea."

Heron shook his head discouragingly. "None around here. I haven't seen one today."

"You don't see ideas," explained Terrapin. "They come inside your head."

Heron gazed stiff-necked down the side of his beak. "If you know where they are why do you bother to look?" he asked listlessly.

Terrapin could not answer this question and so he said, "I think something should be done about big animals. Every time I meet one he tells me how small I am, how big he is and how fast he can run."

"That's nothing," said Heron. "I once met a small bird who told me how big I am, how small he is and how slowly I fly."

Terrapin shook his head violently once more. It felt so over-stuffed with words. Maybe he had got some water in his ears swimming. He shook himself again, but didn't notice any difference. What *had* Heron been saying? Terrapin had no idea and so he said, "Really." It is a word that goes rather well with almost any conversation.

"Yes, indeed," said Heron.

"Is that so?" asked Terrapin, hoping his question would lead somewhere.

"Quite so," affirmed Heron lifting a long leg to scratch beneath his wing. He put down the leg slowly and, opening and shutting his wings a couple of times, worked the ruffled feathers back into place. "Yes, he could fly much faster than I can, but nevertheless I raced him and won. Perseverance counts more than speed. I have perseverance."

Terrapin stretched his neck interestedly. "Did you win a race? I can't believe it. You fly very slowly."

"I have perseverance," repeated Heron. "That's how I won."

"Tell me about the race," said Terrapin.

"It's a long story," said Heron. "I myself am a quiet bird. I lead a quiet life. I should never catch a fish otherwise. In this way I differ greatly from Humming Bird who swoops and darts about with that awful whir of her wings. An annoying little bird!

"Many times I spoke to her about the racket she made and explained how it disturbed the fish and caused them to shun me. I invited her to stay away from the River because the fish thought that I made the noise. But Humming Bird laughed at my invitation and fluttered about my head until I became quite dizzy.

"I asked her to stay among the flowers she loved and leave the River to me which I love. But she said pertly, 'You're just jealous of my wings. They have speed and can beat yours flying anywhere.'

"As you can readily see, this remark coming from the smallest of birds to one of the largest was insulting. For days my appetite deserted me and not even when the fish grew so bold as openly to play about my ankles was I moved to thrust my beak into the water and teach them better manners.

"I thought deeply and when next Humming Bird droned over my head I said to her, 'Will you race me to Stone Squirrel?'

"She laughed saucily and said, 'You can't fly that far. You're too heavy.'

"I repeated my question and she agreed to the race. I made the terms. If she lost, Humming Bird must never disturb me when I'm fishing.

"Stone Squirrel is a great distance from here, but I purposely chose it because after days of meditating I concluded Humming Bird was only a silly little bird and had not my perseverance."

"Perseverance," said Terrapin almost choking over the big word. "Of course she wouldn't have perseverance; Humming Bird's very much too small."

"The race began early one morning. We flew all day. Humming Bird was in the lead, although she made many stops to taste the honey of wildflowers. I was not alarmed because I was behind. This was only the first day and the results of perseverance never appear early."

"Don't they?" inquired Terrapin. "When do they appear?"

"That's another story. Be kind enough not to interrupt this story. At night Humming Bird slept, but I flew on. Until noontime the next day I was in the lead. Then she passed me, flippantly remarking, 'Take care of yourself. Don't get too tired.'

"I paid no heed to her chatter. In the afternoon I passed her a couple of times when she paused for honey and I was greatly encouraged. My perseverance was beginning to take effect. I saw her again in the afternoon fluttering among flower blossoms, but when night came I was still far behind. I kept on flying and hoped Humming Bird was resting for the night. Early next morning I sat on top of Stone Squirrel. Humming Bird was not there. I waited.

"Sometime later I heard her wings buzzing with haste. She was too late. I had won the race. You see, just as I had concluded, she was only a silly little bird with no perseverance. She permitted flowers and sleep to distract her from her goal. Now she doesn't come near the water any more, *thank goodness!*"

"And you won!" exclaimed Terrapin excitedly.

"That was a big race." He thought about it and asked, "Heron, do you think I could win a race from Deer?"

Heron deliberated. "Offhand, I should say no," he said gravely.

"Not even if I make it a long race—say over the Four Hills and if I don't smell the flowers or sleep?" Terrapin persisted.

Again Heron deliberated. "It might be done," he said. "You have one thing in your favor. Deer is a lot like Humming Bird. He is easily diverted, and jumps here and there. But then you're not at all like me. There's something else, though, in your favor. You don't jump at all."

Terrapin crawled briskly toward the water. "Well, I'm going to try racing Deer anyway," he announced determinedly. "You've given me an idea. Thanks very much, Heron."

"I haven't given you anything," said Heron. "The fish are scarce this morning."

Terrapin peered into the River. "That's right, I haven't seen any while you were talking. Good-by, Heron, and thanks for telling me about your race. I've had a delightful morning with you."

"It's not delightful," said Heron. "I've seen better mornings, but the fish may be late. Go quietly, please, in case they're coming up now. Fish have absolutely no perseverance. They frisk about like Humming Bird."

"Good-by," whispered Terrapin.

"Gubble," said the water softly as he slid into it.

Chapter XIV

Terrapin's Trick . .

No one could have been more surprised than Deer, again doing guard duty, when Terrapin bobbed out of the River a few mornings later at his feet, snapped a blithe, "Good morning," and, without waiting for Deer's greeting, brusquely announced:

"Deer, I'm going to race you."

The big animal struggled to hold back the smile that tugged at the corners of his mouth. He did not wish to offend Terrapin and he had been thinking that perhaps he had teased him too much the other day.

"You're going to race *me*, Terrapin?" he asked unbelievingly.

Terrapin cocked his head and looked severe. "Yes," he said. "You won't back out, will you? Remember, you said if I raced you and won you'd go to Black Bear and plead with him to bring Rabbit back from the Island."

"I remember," said Deer. "And you really mean you want to race me?"

"Yes, I'm challenging you to a race over the Four Hills."

Deer gasped and whistled, "Whoo-ee-ee! That's a long course, Terrapin. You can't run so far. Don't you think we ought to have a shorter race?"

"I'm challenging you to a race over the Four Hills," Terrapin said grimly. "Do you accept?"

"But Terrapin——"

"Do you accept?"

"It's too——"

"Do you accept?"

Deer said, "Yes," good-naturedly because Terrapin seemed so unreasonable. They set the time for Friday afternoon at three o'clock.

"Don't forget that you promised to plead for Rabbit's freedom," Terrapin reminded Deer once more.

"I won't forget," said Deer who could not refrain from smiling at the small animal's assurance. Neither could he restrain his banter longer. "With you dashing over the Four Hills, Terrapin, Rabbit is as good as free this minute."

Deer regretted what he said the second it was spoken. He had meant to talk kindly and friendly to Terrapin. The little animal gave him a disdainful glance.

"I know you're making fun of me," he said, "but you'll stop all that when I win the race. I'm going to ask Black Bear to make some rules about how the big animals should treat the small animals."

"I'm sorry, Terrapin," said Deer, truly contrite.

But Terrapin would not talk to Deer again. He dove into the water and swam haughtily away.

As soon as Deer was relieved of guard duty, he sought out Black Bear and told him of Terrapin's challenge.

The two big animals together scratched their heads and wondered, chuckling over Terrapin's audacity.

"I like his spunk," said Black Bear, "but what do you suppose the little dish is planning? Terrapin has never made any trouble for me; he's much too slow for trouble-making. Anyway, I'm glad to see he's Rabbit's true friend. They've been comrades for a long time and Terrapin's probably learned a few tricks from Rabbit. He's up to some mischief. I'm sure we'll all have a good laugh, whatever it is. But I can't imagine Terrapin as a very clever schemer."

Black Bear knew his animals well, but never in the world would he have guessed the scheme Terrapin's small head had thought up. Rabbit, with all his bright tricks, might have been proud of it. Terrapin was even a little amazed at himself.

After leaving Heron at the River Terrapin had spent two days hunting up his four cousins and another day persuading them to help him.

"Why, that would be cheating," they objected at first. "And you know how Black Bear treats cheaters. Oooooo! We'd be afraid!"

"It'll be cheating only if Black Bear finds out," Terrapin argued. "And I don't see how anyone can see through my trick."

"It *is* a very good trick," one cousin agreed.

"Besides I don't care if it is cheating," said Terrapin defiantly. "We're not trying to cheat a small animal. Deer is forty times as large as we are and if we can cheat him, we deserve anything we can get. As my cousins you should be just as mad as I am at the way he teased me. We terrapins have to stick together. Rabbit is our friend and we should be ready to do *anything* for him. Here's our chance to get him out of his prison. I want him back. I miss him so! What would happen if my back were broken again? There'd be nobody to fix it."

The four cousins finally were won over.

"Blood is thicker than water," one of them said.

Terrapin's face puckered in disapproval. "Don't speak of anything being thick," he said. "I'm tired of hearing that word. Thick, small and slow—that's what is forever being said about us terrapins. When we've won this race I shall demand that Black Bear forbid the animals to use them when we're around."

"Then what should I say for what I said?" the cousin asked.

Terrapin thought and suggested, "You could say water is thinner than blood."

"But blood isn't thin. It's thi——"

"Stop!" screamed Terrapin.

The three listening cousins said, "Ssshh!" soothingly because both Terrapin and his cousin were getting nervous and jumpy. They remembered what Terrapin had told them about his conversation with Heron. They were as anxious as Terrapin to win. If they lost Black Bear would surely know that they had cheated and the punishment would be something very unpleasant. But if they should win, the prize would be worth the risk. For they would never again hear those three short, ugly, odious words, thi—, sm— and sl—.

The next morning the five terrapins waddled to the Four Hills to rehearse for the race. When evening came each terrapin knew exactly the part he was to play in the great race which would mean so much to all the small animals. So weary were they, however, that it was decided to spend the night on the spot and be fresh for the morrow. When morning came the four cousins ate a good breakfast, although they were a trifle nervous, and afterward listened to Terrapin who talked to them very seriously.

"Remember now, my cousins, much depends upon you today. I want each of you to go straight to his post, and keep awake, and do not tarry on the way. Remember what happened to Humming Bird. And when you reach your posts be alert and do just what you are supposed to do."

The cousins promised faithfully to carry out instructions, after which the five little animals parted, each trudging off in a different direction. Terrapin himself went toward the foot of the first of the Four Hills where the race was to begin.

He was not the first to arrive there, however. All morning long as the Sun climbed up and up into the blue sky vault, animals, great and small, flocked to the starting place. News of the race had spread through the woods and over the treetops and along the cool, damp banks of the winding streams. For the last few days nothing else had been talked about in Atagahi. And what sport the big animals made of their small friends. A *race* between *Terrapin* and *Deer!*

The little animals answered back as best they could. "Wait, just wait until Friday," they said, "and you'll see a thing or two that will open your eyes."

For all their brave talk not one of the small animals believed in his heart that Terrapin could win. But they turned out loyally to cheer him on. And, oh, if somehow he *could* win, what a splendid thing it would be for all the little folk of Atagahi. They were heartily sick of the big talk and the big airs of the big animals.

Down the trails came the big animals in holiday mood, laughing and jostling one another, and hurling jibes and jests at every little animal in sight. At the starting point they gathered into one group and the small animals into another, and the big animals made the green glades ring with their shouts and merriment.

"Hey!" snorted Panther. "I hear Terrapin once

beat a snail going downhill, and that's why he expects to beat Deer today."

Panther's companions nearly split their sides at this. The small animals looked downcast. They huddled together in silence, for not one of them could think of another word to say. Their courage had all oozed out.

Between the two groups Black Bear stood at his ease, a smile on his kindly face as he listened to the banter and nodded frequently in response to a friendly greeting, first from one group, then from the other. Like the wise ruler he was Black Bear took sides with neither the large animals nor the small ones. Shading his eyes he studied the Sun, now and then, to observe the time of day. Presently he took up a stick and drew a line on the ground to mark the starting place of the race. He said nothing, but all the while shrewd eyes were quietly following Terrapin. What was the little dish up to? Alone of the small animals he was confident.

There he was waiting impatiently for three o'clock when he would race the fastest runner in the woods. He seemed so sure of himself and of victory. At the moment, indeed, he was walking among his small friends, silenced by Panther's sarcastic sally, trying to cheer them up a bit.

"Don't mind what he says," Terrapin said. "Those big, bulky beasts aren't as clever as they think they are. I'll win this race all right. And afterward I think Black Bear will order them to treat us with more respect. They'll never again be allowed to taunt us about being small or slow." Terrapin craned his neck and ran his gaze over the peaks of the Four Hills. "My four cousins and I——" The sentence was not finished. Terrapin's jaws clicked shut and he looked about anxiously, licking his mouth as if he were trying to wipe away the words that had slipped out. "What I was about to say was," he resumed after a pause, "that after this race we terrapins are going to ask that the word thick never be spoken in our presence. And then there's Rabbit. If I win Deer has promised to ask Black Bear for Rabbit's freedom."

"Hurrah! Hurrah!" squeaked the small animals, for they wanted Rabbit back again.

This joyous outburst so surprised the big animals that they had nothing to say in answer.

Black Bear watched and listened to all this, his eyes and ears taking in everything. Terrapin's anxious glance at the summits of the Four Hills, his slip of the tongue about his four cousins made the wise leader wonder. The four cousins of Terrapin: strange they were not here to witness probably the most extraordinary event that had ever happened in the terrapin family. Ah, yes, it was most peculiar. Black Bear's gaze traveled over the Four Hills. "Hmmm," he murmured, as if he were understanding something. Then he ambled slowly over to where Terrapin stood among the small folk and said in a friendly tone:

"Terrapin, that was a nice speech. It was a long speech, too. Should you win—fairly win—this race I shall grant your request. The three objectionable words shall never again be spoken in the presence of sm—, pardon me, Terrapin—in the presence of you or your friends. Perhaps the big animals have had things too much their own way. Undoubtedly their manners could be improved. And as for Rabbit, I think we'd all like to see him back. He has so much fun in him. I really haven't enough to do with him gone. Rabbit's not a very bad rabbit. It's just that he has to learn to obey a few rules. And if you win I'll let you swim to the Island and be the first to tell Rabbit he's free."

Terrapin's Trick

While Black Bear spoke Terrapin stood looking up at him, meeting his eyes resolutely. But he had to blink and swallow when the leader spoke of winning *fairly*. Still he did not retreat and when Black Bear finished talking, Terrapin's gaze had steadied and he said firmly:

"I *shall* win."

Deer took no part in all the hubbub and commotion. He did not join the big animals and gave no encouragement to the taunts they directed at Terrapin. Gracefully he stood off a little distance nibbling at the sweet green grass. Now and again a glossy leaf overhead would take his fancy and, stretching his agile neck, he would clip it off and munch away as if nothing at all were going on.

Black Bear took his place beside the line he had made on the ground and squinted at the Sun.

"It's three o'clock," he announced. "Are the racers ready?"

Deer and Terrapin stepped up to the line. Their friends began to cheer wildly, each group trying to outdo the other.

"Good luck, Terrapin," squeaked the small animals.

"Enjoy your walk, Deer," shouted the big ones.

Black Bear held up his forepaws, stroking downward as he counted, "One! Two! Three! GO!!"

And they were off—up the slope that slanted away toward the crown of the first of the Four Hills.

These hills lay in a wide circle so that the racers having climbed up and down each of them would end their contest where they began it. The slopes of the Four Hills were covered with tall, thick grass, but the summits were as bare as hickory nuts and almost as round.

In this tall grass little Terrapin was lost to view at once, as completely as if he had dived into the River and were swimming on the bottom. And only Deer's bobbing antlers were visible above the waving tops which stirred gently in the wind. Deer was not running his fleetest. No need to do that, surely, in *this* race. But now he approached the bare crest of the first hill. The spectators strained their eyes to catch the first glimpse of him as he emerged from the grass.

But it was not the lithe form of Deer they saw dart from the grass. A little brown speck moved out—and it didn't exactly dart. No—yes—yes, the speck was Terrapin—and he had crossed the bare crest and vanished in the grass on the other side before Deer ever showed himself.

Everyone was too amazed to utter a sound at first. And then as it dawned on the small animals that Terrapin was actually in the lead they found their voices—

and how they found them! But the big animals had nothing to shout about. They stood there in silence, more than a little dazed.

Over the next hill Deer stuck to the course and no glossy leaf diverted him. Still, when he was about half-way to the top, the spectators saw Terrapin clambering over the brow.

Through the tall grass of the third hill Deer's antlers plowed with even greater speed. His friends could tell he was covering long stretches now by leaping more frequently. That should win for him.

"Hurry, Deer, hurry! Only one more hill!" The big animals again had something to cheer about.

But in another moment they were mute and the little animals were shrilling, "Hooray! Hooray!"

Terrapin had gone over the top of the third hill, despite Deer's leaps.

The fourth and last hill and the racers were heading for Black Bear's starting line. Unbelievable as it seems, Deer was able to sprint faster yet. The big animals cheered for all they were worth. Nobody in Atagahi could equal that pace. And just imagine Terrapin trying to! The idea was laughable and so Deer's friends laughed and slapped one another jovially on the back and conceded the race to the big animal.

With long gloomy faces the little animals scanned

the last hill. Deer's antlers slid through the grass. Terrapin didn't have the ghost of a chance and Terrapin's friends weren't squeaking. They were simply waiting for the end. But suddenly Terrapin, fresh as the early dawn and without a puff or a gasp crept from the tall grass which had swallowed him at the beginning and slowly passed over the finish line. And Deer was only half-way down the hill.

The small animals strained their throats yelling with happiness. The big animals were dumfounded. Their mouths were wide with amazement, but not a word came from one of them.

Terrapin was beaming. "Black Bear, I've won!"

"Hmmm," said Black Bear, which didn't sound as if he were offering congratulations.

Terrapin's friends danced about him screaming their praise.

"Hooray! Hip, hip, hooray for Terrapin!"

From him they turned to the despondent group of big animals, skipping impudently before them and reminding them of their humiliation.

"We won! We won! We're the best! We won!" they sang, their little faces grinning with victory.

Deer bounded over the finish line panting, his sleek fur dripping with white foamy sweat. "I've lost!" he gasped, all out of breath from running.

"Well, Deer, what happened to you?" asked Black Bear.

Deer hung his head in shame. "I don't know, Black Bear. I can't understand it all. After the second hill, I ran faster than I've ever run before, but somehow Terrapin managed to keep ahead of me. I've disgraced the big animals. Here are my antlers back."

As Deer began shaking off his crown, Black Bear reached over and held it firmly on his head.

"Now, never mind that," he said. "You ran a beautiful race, Deer, and you keep the antlers. Besides I'll tell you a secret. *You won!*"

Deer gave Black Bear a puzzled look and the leader of the animals snickered. "That funny little Terrapin!" he exclaimed. "He's tried to play a smart trick on us. The silly dish! I'd never have thought him capable of it. But he's been cheating and so I'll have to punish him somehow."

"Oh, don't punish him, Black Bear," said Deer, so happy now that he knew he had not failed the big animals. "He hasn't done any harm. I don't believe he could really ever trick anybody. He's too small. I don't feel cheated. I've had a lovely afternoon racing."

Black Bear smiled. "It's not very serious. Years will pass before Terrapin again gets an idea of this sort. I doubt whether he'll ever have another one." Black

Bear was watching the blissful little animals dancing around Terrapin who was now their hero, and trying to look the part. "It seems a pity to spoil their fun, but I'll do something for them. Let's see, what were the words? Er—small and slow. The big animals will be ordered not to use them in the presence of little animals."

Black Bear sauntered over to Terrapin's circle of jubilant admirers. They were so proud of what he had done! The leader interrupted them with a gruff cough, "Humph!"

Terrapin shot a quick glance at the bear's face. There was something in the tone of the cough that made him uneasy.

"Where are your cousins, Terrapin?" Black Bear asked. "I haven't seen them around today."

Terrapin lowered his eyes. "My cousins," he said hesitantly, "my cousins—why—er——"

"Four Hills," Black Bear broke in and looked at the four crests over which the race was run. Then he looked down at Terrapin and said, "Four Hills, four cousins."

Terrapin's neck began to shorten and his head slid toward his shell. With an effort he stopped its sliding. It was all right to disappear from the animals, but that mustn't happen when Black Bear was speaking. And so the little face remained in sight looking very miserable.

"Well, er—er—I had to win," said Terrapin with a slight sniff. "Yes, it's true; my cousins crawled over each of the hills and I just crawled in and out of the grass down here. But I want Rabbit back and I want a few other things too."

"Cheaters must be punished," said Black Bear sternly. "I'll have to send you to the Island."

Terrapin's neck lengthened and he looked up with excited eyes. "May I go now?" he asked eagerly, adding a delighted, "Oooooo!"

Black Bear bit his lip. He'd forgotten about Rabbit and so picked the wrong punishment for Terrapin. Nothing would please the little dish more than to go to the Island.

"Ooooo," cooed Terrapin again and his four legs took four impulsive steps. "Shall I be off?" He looked disdainfully at the big animals and said, "I'll be glad to get away from all those bullies."

Terrapin's circle of friends was now a circle around Black Bear. While the leader of the animals talked with Terrapin, they had continued to cheer and then they fell to talking over important matters among themselves. Ground Squirrel tugged at the hairs of Black Bear's lower leg to attract his attention.

"Black Bear, Black Bear," she said insistently. "Terrapin won the race. Tell the big animals that we don't like the words small and slow—and Terrapin doesn't like thick—and they must never use them when we're around. Also tell them they must treat us with more respect."

The leader of the animals stared down at the dainty, bright-eyed animal who was sitting up expectantly on her haunches. She was one of the nicest little animals in Atagahi. He felt he could hardly refuse her anything, but of course thick, which Terrapin disliked, could not be chucked out of the big animals' talk; at least, not right now, because, after all, Terrapin had cheated.

"All right, Ground Squirrel," said Black Bear, patting her head with his clumsy paw, "I'll order the big animals never to say small and slow when the little animals are in their company."

"And thick, too, on account of Terrapin," prompted Ground Squirrel.

"No, thick will have to stay because Terrapin did not win his race," said Black Bear.

Ground Squirrel scowled. "What!" she exclaimed indignantly. "Terrapin did win his race. I saw him win!"

"Terrapin did win!" piped up half a dozen small voices.

"No, he didn't," said Black Bear emphatically.

"He did, he *did!*"

"Terrapin——" Black Bear broke off abruptly. His eyes suddenly became aware of a shadow falling across the earth. It wasn't time for nightfall. Could it be—— In alarm Black Bear raised his eyes to the Sun. A big piece of the golden ball was gone!

"The Sky Frog!" roared Black Bear. "Everybody yell and shout! Scare off the Sky Frog! He's eating up the Sun!"

Terrified eyes looked skyward and saw what Black Bear said was happening. The Sky Frog who came about once a year and tried to devour the Sun had already helped himself to a large bite.

Big animals and little animals began a terriffic din to frighten him. This was the way they had been able to save the Sun from the Sky Frog at other times. Black Bear put his hands to his mouth and let out a resounding growl, so powerful it fluttered the leaves on the trees, but the Sky Frog wasn't scared in the least. More of the Sun vanished behind his shadow.

"Louder, louder," urged Black Bear. "We won't have any Sun if the Sky Frog eats him all up."

And each animal thinking how dismal and cold life would be in Atagahi without the bright, warm Sun shrieked with all his might. But it did no good. Some more of the Sun disappeared.

Black Bear went among the animals stirring them up to noisier efforts. He came to Ground Squirrel. She wasn't making a sound and sat sullenly on her haunches with her forelegs crossed on her chest.

Terrapin's Trick

"Ground Squirrel!" exclaimed Black Bear, shocked. "Squeak! The Sky Frog is eating up the Sun. We must save the Sun. Squeak!"

"I won't squeak," said Ground Squirrel stubbornly.

Black Bear caught his breath in dismay. "Won't squeak!" he cried. "Are you out of your senses? Do you realize what it will be like without the Sun? Come, Ground Squirrel, squeak, we need our Sun."

Ground Squirrel tossed her head independently. "I won't squeak," she repeated. "I'd just be helping to save the Sun to make Atagahi a pleasanter place for the big animals. They take everything from the little animals. Why should I do anything for them?"

"I'm not going to squeak either," said Gray Squirrel.

"I won't squeak," said Terrapin.

And the whole group of small animals became silent. With sinking heart Black Bear glanced up at the Sun. Half of him had been swallowed by the Sky Frog. In desperation Black Bear began to argue anew.

"You've misunderstood me," he said. "I promised to order small and slow out of our talk. Surely you can squeak for me. You'll regret it, if you lose the Sun."

"We want thick out too," persisted Ground Squirrel.

With a growl of despair Black Bear ran his paws through the hair of his head, turned and stamped over to the group of big animals. Brown Bear, utterly discouraged, met him and wanted to know what else the animals could do. "We're making no headway at all against the Sky Frog," he said.

Black Bear shrugged his shoulders helplessly and replied it looked as if they were doomed to live in cold and darkness, and then he told how the small animals had refused to squeak.

"Oh, Black Bear, promise them anything," advised Brown Bear. "We'll never again say words they don't like. We'll do whatever they wish."

Black Bear said he thought the little animals had been too disrespectful to be promised anything. Nevertheless, he agreed with Brown Bear. It was more important to all Atagahi that they have the Sun and so he started back toward the small animals to grant their demands. But just before he reached them he was astounded to hear their little voices crying out frightful noises at the Sky Frog. Some of the anxiety and sadness went out of Black Bear's face and a pleased expression appeared instead. They were good little animals after all, Black Bear thought. Their disrespect had not lasted long. In the end they were doing the right thing. Black Bear was proud to be their leader.

"Ground Squirrel, I'm glad you've changed your mind," he said. "Keep up the squeaking. The Sun is nearly gone."

"I didn't change my mind," shouted Ground Squirrel. "Terrapin changed it. He said to forget about thick, and that Atagahi would be a fine place to live in with small and slow gone, but not with the Sun gone. He told us to squeak, but I guess we wanted to anyway. I'd hate not having any Sun."

Black Bear looked around and sure enough there was Terrapin making his share of noise. He said to himself that Terrapin had acted nobly. Black Bear stooped and put his mouth close to Ground Squirrel's ear. "We won't forget about thick," he said. "We'll throw it away with slow and small, but first we must get back our Sun. Yell your loudest, Ground Squirrel."

The little animal smiled and Black Bear smiled and once more everybody was screaming away. But up in the sky the Sun grew smaller and smaller and the Sky Frog stayed. The animals had lost heart and their voices got weaker as their fear increased.

Black Bear strode up and down bellowing, encouraging, but especially he was wondering what more he should do to drive off the Sky Frog. His poor animals! How could they live without the Sun? How could they keep healthy? How could the grass and the trees, that sustained their life, grow? Atagahi would never more be the happy land of the contented animals. Black Bear glanced despairingly at the Sun. The Sky

Frog had most of him now; only a small rim of golden light was there. Without much hope Black Bear rolled out his lustiest roars.

He couldn't hear Terrapin who was standing at his feet calling to him. Finally to gain his attention Terrapin bit his hairy foot.

"Ouch!" growled Black Bear, and bent down to hear what the little dish had to say.

"Black Bear, I've got an idea," said Terrapin. "Why don't you send somebody to bring Rabbit here now? Maybe with one more voice we could scare the Sky Frog off."

The leader of the animals clapped his forepaws together with spirit. "Terrapin, that's a wonderful idea," he said. "I'll send Deer to the Island. He's our fleetest."

In a moment Deer had dashed away and in no time brought back Rabbit.

"Hello, Rabbit, welcome! Come and yell!" the animals cried, making their greeting part of the deafening din directed at the sky.

"Hello!" Rabbit screamed back, and he was so happy to be free that he shrieked at the top of his lungs.

Growling and roaring Black Bear kept his eyes anxiously on the sky. Could his animals save that small band of Sun? The coming of Rabbit appeared to give them new courage and beyond a doubt Rabbit's fresh voice was a big addition to the tumult.

Everyone else was watching the sky too. On other occasions the animals had seen the Sun grow back to his full size, even after the Sky Frog had got away with most of him. In Atagahi the belief was that so long as a tiny part remained the Sun had something to grow onto. The small crescent of light remaining was ever so little, just about big enough to be swallowed with one gulp. Would Sky Frog take this last bite or would the Sun have something left to grow on? Shouts tore the animals' throats. They were making their final try to hold onto their Sun.

Black Bear jerked his head and passed a paw over his eyes. He couldn't be sure, but it did seem to him the crescent wasn't getting any less. He kept his eyes glued to the bright light until it blinded him. He rubbed his eyes, but all he could see were black spots. He rubbed his eyes again, held them quietly closed for a moment and then opened them slowly to the light.

It was true! The Sky Frog's shadow *was* retreating. Black Bear signaled to the animals so they would know the good news. The happy creatures stopped shouting and began to sing and dance.

"Keep up your noise!" thundered Black Bear. "You can't quit yet. The Sky Frog might come back."

Once more the racket started up. This time it did not cease until the Sky Frog was really gone. And he went none too soon either because the animals' voices were gone.

But the Sun full-sized again—his extra large size, in fact, because the afternoon was drawing to a close—shone brightly over the Four Hills. The weary animals sat down to enjoy the lovely sight and to feel the warmth of his rays on their fur coats. It was a wonderful sensation just to lie there stretched out on the grass resting and looking at the lovely light the Sun threw over the earth and the clouds.

The small animals grouped themselves around Rabbit and in hoarse voices whispered how glad they were to have him back with them. Rabbit told them how glad he was to be with them, and no longer an exile among creepy, cackling, disgusting grubworms.

Terrapin finally reached Rabbit's side.

"Oooo, Rabbit, I missed you so much," he whispered. His voice was entirely gone.

"And I missed you too, Terrapin," said Rabbit.

Black Bear marched up to them. Terrapin looked most unhappy. He knew what Black Bear wanted. He had been sentenced to the Island and Black Bear was coming to order him off. He didn't care to go now that Rabbit was back.

"Well, Rabbit," said Black Bear with hardly any voice. "You've been a great help. You and Terrapin have done most today to save the Sun for Atagahi. That was a marvelous idea you had, Terrapin. You were very clever to think of bringing Rabbit from the Island. I am sure he got here just in the nick of time. As your reward, we'll get rid of the word thick. And Rabbit, your reward is your release from the Island. But remember, the two of you," and Black Bear shook a forepaw warningly at them, *"no more cheating."*

Terrapin smiled up at the leader of the animals and nodded his head which meant he promised never again to cheat. Rabbit said, "I'll not cheat, Black Bear."

"You're good animals," said Black Bear and he turned and left them.

"Ooooo," Terrapin gurgled happily. Black Bear had said he was clever. Nobody had ever said that about him.

Rabbit was grateful to Terrapin for getting him off the Island and thought he'd like to do something to please the little dish. He said, "Terrapin, I'll tell you what. I want to see all my friends and tomorrow we'll go calling. I'll stop everywhere you want to rest and I'll tell you all the stories you want to hear."

Terrapin cleared his husky throat and tried to speak. "I don't think we'd better," he said faintly. "Let's wait a few days. I'm too hoarse to call anybody."

Rabbit rolled over on his back and laughed. "And Black Bear was just saying how clever you are," he giggled. "You're the same old Terrapin. Good old Terrapin!"

He sat up and affectionately patted the t—— shell.

THE END